OPTIMAL POWER

CHRIS EDWARDS

ISBN: 978-1-7777761-0-7

Edited by: Stephanie Fysh

Cover design by: Cindy Rose

Layout: Lori Michelle | www.theauthorsalley.com

1

DICE HIT THE pavement in front of Georgia. "It's a six," she said, frowning.

Her friend Felicity beamed. Felicity lay on a grassy rise where the pavement ended, hands behind her head. She didn't need to look at the number Georgia threw, she just knew. She always knew. "You throw a lot of sixes when it snows," she said, pointing past Georgia's shoulder; past the half-demolished buildings, the benches and outhouses, to an old duplex near the west edge of the park. The duplex had a gambrel roof with white trim. It was painted red, like a barn, and people here called it the Barn. There were flakes of snow swirling just beyond it.

"I could throw these dice a dozen times right now and get a different number," Georgia told her.

"But that's not the game. The game is one prediction and one throw. And I can predict what you're going to throw, Georgia." Felicity fluttered her fingers. "I can feel it in the air, I can see it in the sky. Your body radiates the answer."

Georgia did not like the idea that she radiated answers—that waves of true intention pulsed out of her, unbeknownst to her, but easily detectable by her friend. But it had always been this way with the two of them. The day the girls met, Felicity had said she'd seen Georgia in a dream: "Somebody with hair like that," she'd told her, "and eyes like those." She'd sat down on a landscaped boulder in the park and waited for Georgia to show up. When Georgia did, accompanied by her mother, father and brother, plus eight bags of belongings, Felicity bounced into their path to join them. Both girls were eleven. A playmate would be good for both of them, Georgia's mother said.

That was 2070—four years ago. Since then, Georgia had lost track of her mother, father and brother. But Felicity had stuck around. During the winter they hung out together in this park, which formed part of the Annex Winter Relief Space: an artificial temperate zone mandated by federal law for the sheltering of the homeless in cold months. When spring came they left their invisible, immaterial bubble of warmth and lived on the streets of Toronto. And when the cold weather came back they returned to Annex, together. They got by because they had each other.

"What do I win?" Felicity asked. She always forgot the wagering—that was Georgia's department.

"There's nothing I have that isn't already yours."

Felicity propped herself up on her elbows. She looked overhead to a December sky thick with clouds.

"I wish we had a parka," she said. "A big, long, wide parka. One we could both fit into, if we had to. Then we could leave and walk around a bit."

"I hate the cold."

"I hate being bored!" Felicity said. "Who has a coat?"

2

IN THE NORTH END of the park, beneath a large maple tree, sat Otis. He was deep in concentration. In one thick hand he held a small plastic paint roller, attached to a loop of twine; in the other, a twig. He dug into the roller's hub with the twig, dislodging pieces of grit—touching the edge of the roller to turn it, to test it. It moved only a little. Otis grunted, dug some more, flicked two more bits of grit onto the grass. Now the roller turned freely. He looped it around his neck and laid down, resting his naked back against a drawstring bag he'd stuffed with old sweaters, slacks, socks and winter gear. Otis felt the grass on his bare legs; looked up at the green leaves of the maple tree. He closed his eyes and listened to the birds sing.

It was good, he thought, that he'd found this little nook of lawn and shade to lie in this season. It was a slightly depressed piece of land, which afforded anyone who laid low in it a bit of relief from the view around them. It wasn't that the crowds with whom Otis shared this Relief Space were necessarily hard to look at—not on an individual basis. It was the mass of them: the ever-present, oppressive volume of humanity, forced into a space barely large enough to hold them; a space too hot. Always on the verge of terse words or worse. This spot had rarely been free in years' past, but the family who'd typically called dibs on it—and repelled violently anyone who challenged them—had not returned to claim it last fall. Rumor had it they'd owed money to the Casey-Feldmans. Nobody knew for sure, but the family wasn't around to deny it.

Otis was seconds away from a light sleep when Georgia and Felicity arrived. The two girls stood awkwardly by his feet: Felicity with her arm around Georgia, leaning into her slightly, twisting her toe in the sod. The girls were dressed in tank tops and matching faded-pink shorts. Both had small rollers slung around their necks.

"Hi Mr. Colip," said Felicity—she always seemed to be grinning about something. "How's it going?"

"Not bad. How are you girls this fine winter's day?"

"We're bored. We want to go outside."

"In which direction?"

"In whatever direction."

"For how long?"

"For however long," Felicity said. Otis looked at Georgia and the girl smiled quickly.

"Until we get tired," Georgia added.

"So can we borrow your coat?" Felicity dug a hand into her pocket. "We don't have any money, but we won't be gone long, promise. Please?"

Otis pushed himself back to a seated position. "No."

"But you don't need it!" Felicity protested. "You never go out in the wintertime!"

"Suppose I had to. I'll have trouble getting another coat." He wound the string of his clothes bag around his wrist. "Anyway, what if something happened to you two out there? You need a better reason for going out than just boredom."

Were Felicity younger, she'd have stomped her foot. But she was fifteen, so she merely tapped her heel on the grass, once. The big man still noticed. "It's not our fault there's nothing to do here, Otis," she said. "At least you chose to come. We were brought here by our parents."

"The first year, sure. But you keep coming back, every winter, just like the grownups." Otis stood up. He wasn't a tall man—not much taller than the girls even, but he was broad and strong and cut his presence into the air around him. He hauled the drawstring bag up and over his shoulder. "I'm taking a walk," he said. He nodded to the rollers hanging from the girls' necks. "Why don't you go online?"

"The Internet's lame," Felicity said. She turned as he walked by her, calling after him. "You can't hardly get on it anymore!"

3

OTIS HEADED WEST across the parkland, sweating. The heat in Annex had grown oppressive in the last few days—a lung-filling mugginess that sapped its residents of strength. Perhaps that was deliberate: a tactic to keep them docile. But that presupposed that the Canadian government, in its current form, had any capacity for long-term planning. Otis may not have been in the loop like he once was, but he wasn't that naïve.

He'd first come to Annex because it was the largest, best-equipped, and most comfortable of Toronto's Relief Spaces. It covered an existing park in the old Annex neighborhood, plus several more city blocks of repurposed, flattened, sodded and re-planted land to the east, terminating at a stretch of Yonge Street that had collapsed—the old subway tunnel beneath it giving way after years of neglect, on what would have been the 100th anniversary of the opening of the line. Yes, Annex had been the one to beat. But like all the Relief Spaces, it was temporary—so when the warm weather returned Otis had left in search of a job and a new place to live. He found neither, subsisting on handouts through the summer and sleeping on benches and grass while the weather remained good—and in late-Fall he returned to Annex. The Relief Space was no larger than he'd remembered the previous year, but it had hundreds more people in it.

The following Spring was much the same, and so was the one after that. The Relief Space's population kept getting bigger; the job prospects outside remaining slim; the government responding, as always, with austerity measures and lowered taxes. In the third Spring, for the first time, Otis felt unsafe sleeping outdoors in his city. Twice he was attacked— first by two men pushing fifty, just like him, who injured him slightly and took a few of his things. The second time it was one man, younger, clearly desperate, carrying a blade. This time Otis was prepared, and he hurt the man badly. After that, he became very particular about guarding his belongings.

Otis climbed the porch steps of the Barn. He gripped the tarnished door knob while it read his biometric code—everybody had one, unique to them. The lock turned, and the door gave way, opening to a single large room with nothing inside it but crates of supplies and a wide desk in one corner. At the desk sat a slender, athletic man who appeared to have nothing to do.

"Hi Otis," the man said.

Otis sat down. "How goes it, Craig?" he asked, wearily.

"Otis, it's not great; but it could be a lot worse."

Craig Bernhardt was a Life Coach for the Annex Winter Relief Space. He'd been one of twenty-five when Otis first arrived, each tasked with assessing the population's needs and responding to complaints. Now there were seven.

Otis unlooped the roller from his neck and placed it on the desk. "It's nearly dry," he said.

Craig picked up the roller and inspected it.

"Not completely though."

He handed the roller back to Otis.

"There isn't a solid strip of Richpaint left on this thing. If I roll it across this table you'll see streaks. It can't generate a clear image. Should I show you?" Otis brandished the thing before Craig's face.

"Well, no. Then you'd have even less."

"Y'know, when you ripped out the shared terminals last year—"

"They were being vandalized—"

"I know that. I was going to say that I understood that. When the government had them torn out, and you gave us these things, it was with the promise that we'd get refills when we needed them. There aren't a lot of decent flat surfaces to paint in this park to begin with—not when you've got as many people as we've got now, and this paint isn't even good paint! It loses its signal sensitivity ten minutes after you apply it."

"I hear you, Otis."

"Do you?" Otis tapped the desk with his finger. "The Richpaint on here: this is permanent. I know good paint. I worked at *Optimal Power* for 15 years."

"You mean *OP*?" Craig cleared his throat.

"Pardon me. It's hard to keep up with the name changes when your roller's dry."

Craig closed his eyes, inhaling and exhaling slowly, focusing his energy. He opened them again and was renewed.

"The issue, Otis, is supply. I don't have a new Richpaint roller for you because none have been sent to me. And none have been sent to me because their unit cost is high, and, faced with a choice between sending us food rations or improving Internet access, the Government of Canada chose food. Now which would you prefer?"

"How's the Prime Minister eating these days, Craig?"

"Better than either of us, I'm sure. Look: you can blame the government for this if you like. I understand why you would. I understand why most of them," Craig flipped a hand crisply toward the wall that faced the park, "—would do that without a second thought. But you, Otis: You know as well as I do that asking this government to pay out now is pointless."

"I know they're in debt."

"If they were in debt to another country—that would be one thing. But they're in debt to OP. Think about that: the company that supplies the energy that keeps all of us nice and hot all winter long—is owed more than a billion dollars by the very government it's heating. If you're the feds, what do you do?"

"Besides forcing us in here and hoping we die off?"

"Nobody is forcing anything."

"We're being herded, it's more obvious every day." Otis folded his arms on the desk. "A guy I know came back from a trip outside—just yesterday. He tried to return to his old place, which is just a few blocks from where I used to live in the west end. And he just—couldn't. He couldn't get in. Nobody put up any walls. There's no guards or anything. He just couldn't access the place. He says nobody from the Relief Spaces can get in there. Have you heard anything about this?"

"No, no. That doesn't make sense." Craig maintained a baseline nervous tension that made him inscrutable—had Otis even once seen the man at peace, he might've been able to read something in his face now. But no.

"Well, I want to see for myself. I've got stuff outside of here, things that are valuable, that I've had to hide. I buried a box of good-quality tools across the road from my old house. I need to know that I can get to them. Right? If I need money, I can sell them."

"What kinds of tools?"

"Little ones—fine tools, for working on circuit boards."

"Right. Fine. So go. Go get 'em." Craig motioned toward the door. "You have a winter coat."

"That's the other reason I came here. I've got a coat, but my boots are worn through. And so I'm asking my government for a mending kit, so my feet don't freeze." Otis gestured to the crates around them. "We've gotta have some mending kits, right?"

"I have no mending kits."

"Not one kit in all of these crates? What's in them?"

"T-shirts."

"T-shirts?"

"Like mine." Craig patted his chest. His own tee was white with red lettering. 'You Miss 100 Percent of the Shots You Never Take' it read.

"I don't suppose you have boots, then?"

Craig's face fell. One of the frustrating things about him, Otis thought, was how decent he actually was. Were he in a job where some semblance of good work could be done, Craig could have been of great help.

"I have no boots," the Life Coach said, looking at the floor. "No boots for anyone."

4

NEAR THE BARN stood the remnants of a brick wall. It was easy, for someone standing behind this wall, to observe comings and goings from the Barn without being seen.

Georgia gripped an edge of brick, her nose resting on her knuckles, waiting quietly. Felicity, crouched beside her, leaned her head up and out.

"He's been in there a while. What do you suppose he's asking for?"

"Food?" Georgia wondered. She spoke into her hands, so her voice was muffled.

"He probably eats a lot," said Felicity.

The girls kept waiting. Georgia, who was a patient person by nature, maintained her post without much more than the occasional shift from foot to foot. Felicity, who was not patient at all, but knew better how to direct her energy, began making games for herself: counting the number of times Georgia scratched her ear since they'd gotten here, or how many lengths of brick a fat black ant by her head could cross while she held her breath. She became so absorbed in these games that when Georgia hissed to her that Otis had emerged, she didn't hear. Georgia kicked Felicity with her heel, knocking the girl out of her crouch and into the dirt.

"Ow!"

"Shhh, look! He's out. Where's he going?"

Otis was marching purposefully toward the middle of the park, drawstring bag bouncing on his back. He looked agitated.

"Whatever he was asking for—he didn't get it!" Felicity said. "I know where he's headed now. C'mon."

The pathway Otis was taking through Annex was well-worn and familiar to them, and the girls kept just to the edges of it as they followed him along: hopping through old buildings, across new causeways that connected the biggest trees to one another—past a crowd of men circling around two women wrestling for money; past a child's three-on-three soccer match on a small patch of dirt and weeds; over a bathing pool of irregular shape, the trees at its banks forming a canopy over pairs of lovers nestled in private embrace. Always, and everywhere, there were people.

Otis followed the path as it diverted right—around a huge pillar as thick in diameter as four trees. A causeway the girls were running along met this pillar too, much higher—winding around it and continuing upward into the branches. Unable to go further east, they stopped, elbowing their way past people lounging against the guardrail, trying to reach the end of it, following Otis by sight.

Their pillar climbed several stories above the tallest trees in the Relief Space, ending in a disc, more than a hundred feet wide. Its bottom glowed bright white. This disc, one of five in Annex, produced heat. Drawing on Optimal Power, it transformed the air below it into a focused hot zone, overlapping with zones provided by the other four. The disc was warmth, it was life. But that bright white surface, the girls knew, would kill them if they touched it.

They kept sight of Otis until he'd reached almost the end of the Relief Space. That area wasn't quite as crowded, but Georgia and Felicity had been warned not to frequent it. They leaned on the causeway railing, the crush of other people against their backs, watching Otis approach the remains of an old yellow-brick library. A large man—taller than Otis and nearly as wide—stopped him for a moment. Then Otis continued on.

"You see?" Felicity whispered. "He's going to see the Casey-Feldmans!"

Whatever Otis needed, he must've needed it badly.

5

IF THERE WAS something you had to have, you
asked the government for it. Because what the
government gave you was free. But the
government usually didn't have what you were
looking for. So your next stop was the Casey-
Feldmans.

Benny and Briony Casey-Feldman were purveyors
of rare goods (their term): seedy operators for whom
the value of an item was directly proportional to the
desperation of the person needing it. They had stuff
of all kinds hidden in Annex, and more outside it—
held in safes and vaults, covered beneath floor boards,
occasionally submerged. If you needed it, chances
were the twins could get it. But you would pay, and
pay heavy.

The Casey-Feldmans made their base of
operations near the east edge of the Relief Space, on
a shabby patch of cement, shrubs and skinny trees
called Town Hall Square. Its distinguishing feature
was its rows of yard-high concrete planters, molded
into the shape of flower pots. For some reason, only
small tufts of hedge had ever been planted in these
planters—hedges that could've been served by a pot a
fifth the size of the planters—which were, of course,

about five times the size of a regular pot. It was a design choice worth pondering. And people might well have pondered it—perhaps from one of the old wooden benches situated on the north side of the square, Otis thought, as he passed them—if the square were a safe place to hang out. But it wasn't. The only people who lingered on those benches were the heavies in the Casey-Feldmans' employ, and they didn't cotton to the uninvited. As for the giant pots: they proved handy to hide behind, and beyond that, the Casey-Feldmans didn't give a damn about them.

"Boots?" Briony asked Otis.

"Where have you got to go that's so important?" asked Benny.

Otis knew better than to give the twins that much information. They had received him as they always did, sitting side-by-side on a large stack of blocks made of sawed and resewn pieces of upholstered furniture, upon which had been piled a dozen or so pillows and cushions, inconsistent in shape, color and construction. Otis stood at the foot of this throne, peering up.

"I'm tired of being in here," he said. "It's too cramped. I need to get out and move around. So I need warm boots. You already said you didn't have a mending kit."

It was a funny thing about the Casey-Feldmans that they looked nothing alike. Benny was a fine-boned young man with a prematurely old bearing, with tiny gray eyes and high, sharp cheekbones that seemed to draw the lines of his face upward. Briony was short and plump, with large eyes set in a fleshy, round face that appeared jolly, or would have, if you knew nothing about her line of work.

"Got anything to trade, Otis?" Briony asked.

"No—nothing I don't need. But I do have money." Otis motioned to an open spot of cement near his feet. Briony nodded, and then he knelt, running his Richpaint roller over it.

The texture of the cement was not ideal for this purpose, nor was Otis's roller, which gave up nearly its last dregs of Richpaint, leaving a streaky path about a foot long. He pressed his fingertips on the painted surface and after a moment was able to draw up a flickering, fractured holographic display.

"That's your bank account?" Benny asked, grinning coldly.

Otis angled the image toward himself, so the siblings couldn't see it so clearly. There were a lot of numbers in the columns but none of them had more than two digits. And they were shrinking, because, while the government described the Winter Relief Spaces as charity, it still extracted a nominal fee from those living in one.

"Rates are volatile, aren't they?" said Benny. "You can never be sure what you're worth."

Otis nodded.

"Still, we can help you," Briony said. "Boots are easy enough to find." She looked upward, wistfully, and squinted, although it was still overcast. She liked to appear magnanimous. "But just because boots are easy to find, that doesn't mean they're easy to smuggle. Boots are bulky, for example."

Otis tuned out the rest of Briony's spiel. He was familiar with it, and knew it offered nothing to the prospective client, only to the seller, who wished to hear herself heard.

"—and given that risk," Briony droned, her

brother nodding at predetermined intervals, "we can't sell you a pair of boots, before the end of the season, for less than 400." She flicked an invisible midge off her arm. "I'm told that a new pair of boots retails for 2,000 outside."

"I'd heard 2,500," Benny added.

"I can pay 400."

The twins smiled in unison. Benny produced a flat wooden tablet, Richpainted like Craig's desk. He tapped it a couple of times and it glowed silver. He had the big guard hand it to Otis.

Good paint, Otis thought, admiring the tablet's smooth coating. He touched a green marker on the surface and instantly his account was 400 lighter. He returned the tablet to the guard.

"Pleasure doing business, Otis," Briony said. As she spoke her brother climbed down behind them and reached into a large bin. He pulled out a pair of heavy work boots, tied together by the laces, and lobbed them toward Otis—they spun through the air and Otis caught them easily in his left hand. He did not try them on—whether they fit properly or not, they would have to do. They'd cost him all the money he'd had left.

6

ANNEX HAD NO formal boundary—no checkpoint, no wall. There was simply a point beyond which the discs ceased projecting enough energy to keep things comfortable. You noticed it gradually—if you walked in any direction long enough you'd find the temperature starting to drop; the flowering plants around your feet would darken, then grow sparse; the tree branches would be thinned of their leaves. In the course of these observations you would be forced to tuck in your arms, then hurry your steps, then don a coat—then more.

Otis's boots fit. He'd put them on as he approached the Relief Space's southwestern edge, about a block north of Bloor Street, then added a thick parka, a knitted toque and a pair of woolen mitts. All this, plus his bag of clothes, had given him a lumpen, indefinable appearance—one he hoped would limit questions rather than encourage them. It wasn't good for an Annex dweller to draw too much attention.

He lumbered westward on Bloor, along unplowed sidewalks, the street empty but for the regular rumbling-past of light-rail trains, running on a track cut through its center. The trains were lines of dingy green boxes, their windows shuttered to keep out the world. The track below them glowed bright white, just like the underside of the discs.

He came to a boarding station at the corner of Bloor and Spadina Road. A Plexiglass-type shelter, accessible by a set of sliding doors. Touched a red circle to the left of the doors, hoping they would open. They did not, of course—Otis couldn't afford a train ride. He stood there, scowling, till the paying customers inside became aware of him, and began looking at him with suspicion—or pity, perhaps, which was even worse. He moved on.

He continued walking for more than two hours. Bloor became more dangerous past Christie Street, so at that point he headed northwest, cutting through parkland and into residential areas whose prosperity had risen and fallen, suddenly and repeatedly, over the last few years. Rows of three or four houses were separated by long stretches of unused land, where other houses had once stood before being sold, below cost, or simply abandoned with goods still inside, to developers, who then demolished them. Sometimes these voided properties lined up, so that Otis could peer across many blocks at once. It was through one of these gaps that he saw the sludge-gray concrete pillars of a multilane thoroughfare, constructed, in 2045, to convey traffic from the Lakeshore directly to the high-rise developments being built north of here. The high-rises were never completed, and federal funding for the thoroughfare disappeared. Thirty years later it remained unfinished—a public-works project too expensive to complete or tear down; incapable of easing travel, as was its purpose, yet effective at redirecting around it any traveler who wished to continue across its land and deeper into the west end.

Otis kept on, till he'd gone past the point where construction had been halted. The housing here was spotty, as it had been earlier, and for the same reasons. The same developers, even. Those developers couldn't profit from the land they'd bought so cheap, and so, one by one, they'd failed—selling their assets to corporations, like *OP*, that could afford to buy them. It was said that *OP* had one of the country's finest private art collections—the result of a compulsive buying spree lauded by some as a godsend, since museums lacked the resources needed for preservation. It's good, Otis thought, as he crunched through snowdrifts topped with frost, that somebody's saving the art. The artists might freeze to death, but their work will survive. The artists he'd known would be fine with that.

7

HIS **OLD HOUSE** was in a Toronto neighborhood called the Junction, on the northeast corner of Junction Road and Keele Street, a dozen blocks from *Optimal Power*'s National Headquarters. The skyscraper gleamed in the distance as Otis walked down Keele, its teal-glass body flanked by pairs of mammoth power generators colored indigo and ash-gray. The employees of *Optimal Power* had congregated around these buildings, morphing the area from a light-industrial one into something tony and residential. Even those on the second-tier, if they were valuable, skilled employees, like Otis had been, were offered space in the new hub. He'd lived here, in a cozy, two-story house, for years. Even after *OP* let him go, he stayed. It was his home until the day Angie threw him out.

The bundle felt heavy on his back. Otis slung it down and flexed one arm so he could swing it as he walked, moving it in front and behind him like a pendulum as he approached the corner. But the nearer he got, the harder this became to do. For a moment he thought it was fatigue, but as he pressed on the stress on his arm increased to an unnatural degree, until it was as though he were moving the bundle through water. His legs were obstructed too—no, not obstructed, resisted—and as he drew close enough to his old house to distinguish the contours of white upon its roof, where the snow had settled and frozen—at about that point—his strength became inadequate to the task of reaching it.

Otis dropped his bag in the snow. Extended his hands into the invisible thick-soup. Leaned forward, into seeming-thin air, head-first, and hung, at a 45-degree angle, without falling. There was no hope.

He picked up his bag and backed away. With every step he felt less impeded—and more welcome. The smaller the house became, the freer his body.

8

"WHAT YOU WANT will cost 5,000," Briony told him, the next morning. "You're asking us for a hacker, you realize that? Someone who can tether your biometric code to a higher Certification of Access, so the Bog that *OP*'s got set up in your old neighborhood doesn't recognize you. We can find that person. We know several. But you can't afford it. So what do we do?"

"Cut me a break?" Otis ignored a smirk from the Casey-Feldmans' guard.

"Ha! No." The Casey-Feldmans said 'no' in unison, which added a layer of comedy to Otis's predicament. "Your only option is to work it off."

"I'm not beating people up for you."

"Naturally," Benny sneered.

Briony tapped her brother's arm playfully. "He's always been too nice, Benny. That's his trouble."

"So what other morally-compromising task can we set you on?" Benny asked. "I think we'd like you to rob a few homes. Nothing violent—necessarily. Just get in and get out with whatever you can carry. Which is—" Benny motioned to the various proofs of Otis's brawn—"probably a lot."

"You don't have enough thieves already?"

"You can never have too many thieves," Briony informed him. "And we prefer 'partner'. We're team builders, in the old-school sense of the term. We give people a reason to invest in the work they do." She sized up her new recruit, filling with pleasure as she did so. "Your old neighborhood still has people in it, Otis; money. That's a lucky break for you. So clean it out!"

It took the Casey-Feldmans three days to deliver.

People with whom Otis dealt during those three days described a man even gruffer than usual; more to the point; even less willing to entertain any point that might distract him from his brooding. But he told no one what was bothering him. At the close of the third day, as Otis sat dozing under his tree, the string of his clothes bag wound twice around his arm, the Casey-Feldmans' huge guard appeared over him.

"It's done," said the guard. And that was that.

9

OTIS'S NEXT TRIP out of the Relief Space was late that night. He'd left his clothes behind, in the Barn, Craig promising to watch over them, carrying only the bag. He reached the Spadina boarding station just as a train was arriving. This time the sliding doors of the shelter opened for him. Whoever it thought he was, that person could afford to take transit.

The train car was empty. Otis landed heavily on the middle seat in a row of three, facing the opposite side of the vehicle. The car trembled, then began to build speed, the ride smoothing as it did so, Otis relaxing along with it; he took his bag out of his lap and rested it on the seat next to him, drinking in the interior of the train car, a bland green decor matched to the exterior, but still, for him, fresh and exciting. It had been a long time since he'd ridden public transit. Otis looked at the shuttered windows and smiled. It'd been a long time since he'd been able to shut out the world.

Two thefts, maybe three. Otis was sure he could rob a few big houses and be done with his debt to the Casey-Feldmans. There were lots of big houses in his old neighborhood—he'd lived in one himself. Not huge, of course—he wasn't the ostentatious type and neither was Angie. Just big enough to make a man feel comfortable; to give him the space he needed to stretch out, be alone; to unwind after a long and stressful day. And for Angie too, who'd been a painter, and still was one, and who needed a studio, and who'd expanded that studio from a single room on their second floor to three rooms, her work gaining notice, as it rightly should have, until Otis, home for days at a time once *Optimal Power* let him go, was practically tripping over works of art on his way to the toilet—

The shriek of old brakes pulled Otis from his thoughts. The train stopped, the doors to his right hissing open, letting another passenger on the train. He was a man about Otis's age, wearing a top coat over a brown suit. He stepped quickly into the car, found a seat nearly across from Otis, but not quite; produced from his coat a wooden tablet, letting it rest on his lap, and began moving a set of orange icons from one side of the holographic display to the other, much as he would have an abacus. The man looked up for a moment, smiled politely at Otis, then returned to his display.

What this man was up to, in here, at this hour? Otis watched him work—the images on his tablet crisp, the surfaces solid and the colors deeply saturated and pure. Not like the ragged-edged, washed-out graphics you got from a government-issued Richpaint roller. This man was wealthy, Otis thought. Then he corrected himself. No, this man might not be wealthy at all; it was simply that Otis was poor.

Keele Boarding Station, an automated voice announced. The man shut off his display. The train slowed, he and Otis standing up at the same time.

"Well," said the man, tucking his tablet into a leather sleeve, "have a good evening." He gave Otis a salute and parted through the open door, into the night.

"Good evening," Otis said, too late to be heard.

10

HE EMERGED FROM the train only four blocks from his old home. Scraped snow off the pavement in front of the Plexiglass shelter, sliding his roller over the cleared patch—enough to get a few streaks. Brought up his bank account and selected Personal Information.

The hack was thorough: access to public spaces marked FULL; access to residential spaces marked not with a single address, or even several, but with a digital blur: the address of every house and apartment in this neighborhood appearing, disappearing and reappearing at a rate of 10,000 listings per second—many times the actual number of houses in the area. It created a degree of overlapping access coverage faster than residential security software could keep up with. Only corporate properties could keep him out now.

The Optimal Power Bog, as Benny Casey-Feldman called it, began halfway between St. Clair Avenue and Junction Road—near the beginning of a wall made of rough-hewn, white stone. As Otis approached this wall he thought, as he often had, about the illusion of it: its top a series of flat blocks, descending southward like long steps, but the grade of the street, which declined more sharply, making it seem as though the wall were growing taller instead. This wall had fascinated Angie.

As Otis drew near to his old house again he tensed up. Clenched the neck of the drawstring bag and walked faster, shuffling through heavy snow; huffing clouds of breath as he went. Trying to build momentum. But this time there was no resistance. He reached the house, then scrambled up the side of a little hill across the road from it, his short legs sinking in the drifts, stopping only when he stood level with his old bedroom window. The window was lit, but the blind was drawn and there was no movement behind it. Otis waited, just to make sure.

They'd picked this house the first day Junction Road was made open to *Optimal Power* employees. It was a long building, with tall windows, comfortable for more than two. The grade of its roof descended gradually, in a series of long steps, like the white wall on Keele Street did. But since Junction Road rose from the corner, the house seemed to taper toward a point as one looked left to right—a subtle element, providing compositional unity across the Keele-Junction intersection. You could see this if you stood where Otis did right now, but he'd never noticed it until Angie sat him down and pointed it out. He'd gotten better about noticing such things.

All remained quiet behind the blind. Satisfied that he wouldn't be seen, Otis began digging, scooping big handfuls of snow with both hands and depositing them to one side. Angie wasn't in that house, he knew that much. She'd put it on the market in the first year of the Relief Spaces—he'd wasted a lot of time lined up at the Annex shared terminals, so he could read the listings. Where she'd gone after that he didn't know, though exhibitions of her work were still being held. Does it matter where a great artist lives? Otis wondered, as he reached the soil. All that matters is where the art is. He opened the drawstring bag and removed a piece of curved metal he'd scavenged. Hacked away at the frozen ground, again and again; until the dent in the earth became a hole; until the edge of the tool clanged against something solid. He brushed cold dirt away from the bit of exposed material, then continued working.

It took more than a half-hour to extract the object from the ground. When he was done, Otis had in his lap a slim copper tool box, sealed with two clasps. He ran his fingers over its smooth edges, tracing the bulges of its hinges, the lines of the clasps; forgetting the winter, and everything else.

Feeling, for a moment, like a man worthy of such a possession.

11

MURRAY VAN DYCK had lived up the road from Otis and Angie, in a nice house at the end of Junction. Like most of their neighbors, Murray was an *Optimal Power* employee, working in Accounting. He had been a decent, if annoying companion, who borrowed too often, Otis thought, and deserved a more assertive wife. But Murray and Magda had been the first to welcome them to the neighborhood, and that had meant a lot to Angie.

Otis stood on the sidewalk in front of the Van Dyck's darkened house. Casing it, he supposed. He snuck around to the far end of the garage, where he knew there was another door, and grabbed the handle. Instantly the lock released. Creeping across the dark interior of the garage he reached another door, leading to the laundry room. The laundry room was dark, the house silent. Otis went as quietly as he could. By the time he reached the living room he knew the Van Dycks didn't live here anymore.

Murray and Magda had both been collectors, and their collections were missing. Otis touched a dimmer switch on the wall, nudging it till the lamp overhead cast a faint glow across the living room, revealing the rows of wall shelving where Magda had arranged her more than 200 pairs of salt and pepper shakers. The shelves were still there but the shakers were gone, replaced by fitted blocks of various sizes. The blocks were cast in primary colors, forming a pattern that reminded him of Mondrian.

Magda's shakers had occupied one wall of the living room, Murray's vintage books almost the whole of the other three. There were no more books here either. Now those shelves held photos. More than a hundred, Otis guessed, most of them posed portraits. Many in black-and-white. He squinted at the images in the dim light. The men and women looked weathered and hard, their faces stern, their postures formal, the clothing they wore fitted and stiff. Everything about the photos was rigid, inflexible, and joyless.

Otis and Angie had spent a lot of time in this room. It was where the Van Dycks entertained, which for Murray, at least, involved showing off. Though he wasn't a subtle man, Murray'd had a gift for inserting news of his wealth into casual conversation, and so Otis had learned of the Van Dyck's new boat, for example, not by taking a ride on it, but by being offered a glass of pricey scotch from a distillery Murray had discovered on one of his trips along the water.

Whenever Murray had exited this room to get the men another couple of drinks, which was often, he would run a fingernail along the leather spines of his volumes. Fip-fip-fip. That noise had irritated Otis. Fip-fip-fip. That and a hundred other little things Murray did, week after week, year after year—an obnoxious aggregation that crowded out his other, more defensible qualities. Till it seemed that the only reason to keep a friendship with him was that one already existed.

He picked up one of the photos. It was a family portrait with seven children, the children lined up in a row, from tallest to smallest, with an infant in its mother's lap at the terminus of the line; the father projecting a severity from the other end that the little ones seemed to absorb. Frame's heavy, Otis thought. Looks like silver. A lot of these frames looked like silver. He opened his drawstring bag and began placing the old photos into it, as fast as he could. Soon he'd nearly cleared one wall, taking every frame that looked valuable, barely glancing at the pictures in them as they disappeared into his bag, quietly as he could.

As he pillaged, he thought back to the day that he and Murray finally fell out. It began on a Tuesday, six years ago, when Otis spotted Murray and two colleagues approaching him in the hallway at work. Well, not approaching him exactly—just walking in his direction, absorbed in a mutual exchange of Accounting jargon, not even noticing Otis ahead of them. Otis had stopped and turned as they passed him; Murray locked eyes with him for a moment and kept on going, not even acknowledging his neighbor.

Otis could have strolled up the road that evening and confronted Murray about the snub. But instead he waited, until the next time Murray showed up on his porch, looking for something to borrow. Murray opened his mouth and Otis held up his hand, guiding him to the back deck—perhaps too firmly, Otis thought later—and told him off.

Murray explained that he'd been preoccupied that

day. The people he'd been walking with were Accounting executives, and the topic they'd been discussing was a sensitive one—probably not suitable for a hallway, now that he thought about it—and they wouldn't have appreciated Murray breaking stride to talk to a colleague from Robotics, even if that colleague was also a good friend and neighbor. He hoped Otis understood. Otis didn't, but he forgave Murray anyway. Three weeks later, he was fired. Not for any misdeed, and certainly not for incompetence, the Occupational Transition Specialist assured him. It was simply that Otis's role, like the roles of all his colleagues in Robotics, was no longer deemed essential. Murray didn't show up to borrow anything after that. In fact, the two men never spoke again.

Otis cleared the second wall of silver frames, brass frames, finely-grained wooden frames, moving onto the third. On these shelves there were more color photos, but he dumped them in the sack just as briskly, keeping an ear tuned for noises in the house, hearing none. He was halfway down the shelves on the third wall when one of the photos caught his attention. Made him stop.

It was a picture of a young couple and their daughter. The father and mother were kneeling on either side of the little girl, grinning; she stood between them, smiling wide, front teeth missing, holding up a plaque of some kind. It was a warm picture, loving and casual, unlike the older ones. Otis saw that the little girl's legs were bent and slack. She was not standing. Her parents cupped their hands behind her, supporting her weight.

Further along the shelf were more pictures of the

couple, looking older, more serious. He saw no more of the little girl.

Otis set the bag down. He widened it so it sat slack on the floor, surrounding the pile of framed photos inside. Took out the first ones, picking at the clasps on the backs of them, nudging out the old photos, then setting them back on the shelves in the first wall. He did this for the second wall, and the last; working slowly so the delicate images would not be damaged, listening all the time for sounds of movement.

When he'd placed the last of the photos back on the shelves he drew the bag shut. There was nothing else in the room worth taking, so what now? The second floor seemed risky. The kitchen? Yes, he would check the kitchen and then leave, quietly, as he'd come in. The kitchen was down a hallway to the right. Otis left his bag in the living room, stepping into the hall. But he did not go further.

In the hallway, set in a recessed circular mount within the wall, was one of Angie's paintings. One of the 'speed paintings' that had made her a sensation.

The painting was disc-shaped, a little bigger than a dinner plate. It depicted a young couple, in 19th-Century peasant dress, sitting together. The man in the picture was burly and serious; he sat straight on a wooden stool, one arm around his wife; the other resting on his lap, fist balled over one knee. The woman was slight; she seemed swallowed by her husband's girth, her expression bleak. She wore a simple pink dress, faded almost white, contrasting the man's rich red smock.

She must've painted this one after I left, Otis thought. He scanned the painting, looking for its key. A speed painting was not one work of art, but two—

press the key, hidden somewhere within the still image, and the painting's components would rearrange themselves, the whole of it beginning to spin. You would see another image appear. Angie always said that her speed paintings were in conversation: the first image was a question answered by the second.

He found the key, but did not press it. The painting's question was not one he wanted answered.

Instead he found his length of metal again, using it to pry the painting out of its mounting. Slinging it under one arm he returned to the living room, placing the painting in the bag. He extinguished the light, lifting the laden bag, with the frames and the painting and his copper box all clamoring inside—and then overhead, as if in response, a floorboard creaked. Otis froze. He heard another floorboard bow, and then another, and then he raced to the garage.

12

"ONE HUNDRED," said Benny. He tossed the last frame over his shoulder; it landed with a clank in the bin. "For all of it."

"Are you kidding me?" Otis made the beginnings of a motion toward Benny, then the Casey-Feldmans' guard made the beginnings of a motion toward Otis, who stayed put.

"Don't tell us what's fair, Otis," Briony said. She sat calmly while the men repositioned themselves. "You've delivered less than we expected. Less volume of product; less value per unit."

"Some of those are silver, you know."

"I know that, Otis. But I don't know what we'd do with a pile of old picture frames."

"Melt them down." Otis's back ached from the previous night's work. He was tired. He'd slept only a couple of hours after returning to Annex. He let his bag rest on the pavement next to him, the speed painting and the copper box still inside.

"We might find somebody who could do that," Briony said. "But that's extra work on our part."

"True," Benny said, grinning. "Make it seventy-five."

"I want you to pay off this debt, Otis," Briony

continued, her voice thinning. "You're someone worth keeping around." The Guard grinned, just like Benny, Benny noticing and chuckling—only Briony and Otis seemed to be taking this seriously. "Just bring us things we need. It's that simple. Equipment, tech. Or survival stuff: Cushions, blankets. Do you understand?"

Otis looked down at the bag. "What about art?" he asked. "I picked up a speed painting last night."

"Is that something you paint real fast?"

"No, it's—" Otis tapped the sack with his heel, shifting the contents. "It's a painting that looks like one thing, but when you touch a certain spot, the parts of it shift around, and spin, and then you see something different. The painter's very talented. She's respected, and famous. It's probably worth a lot."

The twins chewed on this for a moment.

"Famous can be bad," Briony said. "It's hard to fence." She glanced at her brother, who gave her nothing in terms of a response, at least that Otis could decipher. But it did seem like there'd been communication. "We might take it for three hundred. Though god knows when we'll get rid of it."

Otis did not thank her. He simply dug into his bag, found the painting, and handed it up to Briony, image-side down.

"What's wrong, Otis?" she asked him, flipping the painting over so she could see it. "Not your taste?" She glanced at the peasants in the painting, then back at him. Her eyes widened, but she said nothing more. Benny didn't bother to look.

13

OTIS RETURNED TO his old neighborhood the following week. This time he avoided Junction Road, choosing a nearby street with bigger houses. The street was dark, save for the glow of the lights on the porches of the homes, or over the garages, but there was a full moon overhead.

He found an old house set well back from the sidewalk. Crossing a long pathway of paved stone he drew near the porch, stepping onto the snow-covered lawn to avoid the breadth of the porchlight's beam; scrambled onto the porch without using the steps; grabbed the iron knob on the front door—hoping the locking mechanism was modern, even if it appeared otherwise. After a long second it clicked, and the knob loosened. Otis slipped inside, shutting the door quickly behind him.

The door led to a small cloakroom with a wooden bench and mirror, separated from the rest of the house by a second set of doors, made of frosted glass. These doors gave way just as the front door had, shuddering slightly as Otis opened them—he was careful to do this gently, to avoid any sound. He was looking down a long hallway now, his eyes drawn to a small wooden table at the end of it, bearing a marble statue of a cat, brightened by moonlight through a window.

That statue looked valuable. And it was portable. Otis moved toward it, the old floorboards whining beneath him. From the corner of his eye he saw a large staircase, deep and curved, leading to the second floor. He stopped. There's something on those stairs, he thought. Something in the shadows. A woman.

She stood halfway down the staircase. She wasn't moving. Otis could make out only the outline of her— her shoulders hunched as though she were carrying something.

"I'm sorry," he murmured. "I'm lost."

The woman did not respond.

Otis wondered what to do. This was bound to happen of course—how could he not have an excuse, a backup plan, to deal with it? He should just leave; hoping the woman could see him no more clearly than he could see her. Hoping she wouldn't call the police.

But what if she wanted to? How could he stop her from doing that?

"I won't hurt you," he said. And then, a little louder: "I'm not a thief." But the woman said nothing, still did not move.

With deliberate, demonstrative motion, Otis set down his bag. He knelt, again slowly, unlooping his Richpaint roller from around his neck, making short, furtive strokes across the oak floor, managing a weak imprint. From the paint he drew up an image of a government homepage—faint and flickering, but bright enough that it illuminated part of the staircase above him, and the woman upon it—

—who was not, as he'd begun to suspect, a woman at all.

She was another statue. A stone sculpture of a woman, carrying a young child in her arms.

The staircase was thickly carpeted and Otis made no sound as he approached the statue, stopping on the step below it, looking at the intricate stone folds of its dress; the curls of hair on the infant's head; the statue's delicate feet on their stone base—the base planted firmly on the step. The statue's posture was that of a woman taxed bodily, as though she were weary, and the child, heavy. Her face was resolute; her eyes wide, but blank.

What was the statue doing here? Otis wondered. It was unlikely it could have fallen to this spot. The steps above were undisturbed, and surely they would not have been, if such a weight had bumped down them. But who would place something like this in the middle of a staircase? Unless it was a marker of some kind: a reminder to stay out of the upper floor. Perhaps there were renovations being done up there, perhaps there was damage. It seemed overkill to place a piece of art here instead of, say, a chair. But people could be odd about such things, especially in their own homes.

He stepped around the statue and up to the second floor. The carpeting continued, muffling his footsteps, leaving no trace of him as he walked the railed edge of the hallway, looking down at the Richpaint strip still glowing near the front door. There were several bedrooms on this floor, the doors of each one slightly open, Otis nudging each of them open a little wider as he passed by, the hinges not making a sound. The bedrooms were empty. There was a bathroom too, its fixtures intact, but absent any signs of regular use.

Otis followed the railing until he reached the last of the rooms, by size and position likely the master bedroom. This time the door was shut. He could open it quietly too, he was sure. And then he would know what was inside—if only so he could move on, without exploring further. He touched the doorknob gingerly, turning it slowly, and the door gave way.

He felt an immediate chill. The room was dark but for the moonlight, and unoccupied like the rest, but there was a queen-sized bed in it, and beyond that an open window. Otis entered, passing between the empty bed and the wooden bureau at the foot of it, tugging the window closed and locking it. The bed seemed to be in use, or at least had been. The sheets and blankets on this side had been tugged down, away from the pillow, resting in a rumpled heap about where a person's feet would have been, as though that person had flung off the covers and lurched out of bed. This unmade bed was the only sign of life Otis had seen in the house.

There was more. Beside the bed, standing level with it, was a bassinet. Inside was a stuffed doll. The doll lay facing the bed, its limbs rounded, puffy stumps, its head a soft ball with stenciled eyes and mouth, and yarn strands for hair. The whole setup was unsettling, Otis thought, but there was a glimmer here of something more; a signpost, maybe, that his distracted mind ought to be focusing on. If he wasn't here to rob, perhaps; if speed didn't matter, he would give it more thought.

He walked around the bed, to its undisturbed side, near the door. Sat down, feeling the comforter, smooth and cool, beneath his hands. Let his fingers sink deep into it. Oh, it was softer and more giving than the softest earth, Otis thought, better than the thickest patch of grass. He wanted to lay back, let his heavy body relax. But he could not. This was a room full of treasures, maybe. Things the twins wanted. Clothing, bedding—

He moved from the side of the bed to the foot of it, with the bureau in front of him, and pulled open one of its wide drawers. Inside was a thick, cream colored blanket, sheets and pillow cases. Otis dug his hands into the drawer, drawing the blanket up to his face. 'Survival stuff', Briony had called it. The blanket felt cozy, smelled fresh. Better than fresh: like lilac fabric softener. He dug in again, pulling out more bedding, wriggling and nestling his fingers in the soft folds of it like a child. Then he touched something hard. At the very back. Otis reached in deeper, flicking it and feeling it spin on one side. He knew this shape. It was the shape of something rare in this world. Something valuable and deadly.

Otis withdrew a pistol from the drawer. He sat looking at it, feeling the weight of it in his hand, incredulous. He did not know much about guns. He'd fired one once, at a target range—a rifle, not a pistol. He hadn't enjoyed the experience, telling Murray, who'd been the one to invite him, that he felt safe enough without guns in his life. 'Who'd mess with you anyway?' Murray replied.

Otis took hold of the black plastic grip. Pointed the pistol toward the far corner of the room, putting the barrel as far from him as he could reach. His fingers explored it, the straight and flat planes of its surface, functional and artless. He was aiming at nothing; trying very hard to imagine nothing in front of him.

There was a little black button near the trigger

guard. He pressed it and the end of the pistol's magazine popped out of the grip. He drew out the magazine, a slim rectangle lined with a double row of small circles along one side and a golden bullet peeking out of its top. The gun felt very light without its bullets.

Now Otis let himself imagine targets. Some of them he was ashamed of even considering, others he was sure he was justified in wanting shot, though he would never do it. The faces of the men and women who'd wronged Otis Colip flitted through his mind's eye, projected over that drab and featureless corner of the room, all of them at point-blank range. He squinted, feeling suddenly in character—brought the pistol closer, turning it sideways, pressing his other hand over the top of it, like he'd seen done in old movies, sliding the top of the gun backward.

Another bullet fell out of the gun, into his hand.

He lowered the pistol quickly—sure, but still not sure enough, that the thing was harmless. But guns were never harmless. He would leave this one here.

No! He would sell it.

This was a near-instantaneous shift of opinion, unmotivated by deeper thought, and it surprised Otis. For a moment he felt disassociated from it, from the part of himself that thought it. But yes, as the seconds ticked by and the opinion established itself, he grew more at ease with it—the idea of taking the pistol from this house, of selling it to the Casey-Feldmans for a massive sum, the twins then reselling it, perhaps to someone outside Annex, who might need it. Someone smaller than Otis, who might need protection more than he did. He found his bag and filled it fast, the cozy bedding nuzzling the pistol and its magazine and bullets and the copper box, and got the hell out of that house.

The next afternoon he visited Benny and Briony, selling them the entirety of the bedding. But when he got to the bottom of the bag, to where the gun and the magazine had descended, he said nothing.

14

OVER THE NEXT few weeks Otis made nine trips to the old neighborhood. He targeted one house each night, encountering no resistance, no heightened security measures, and so far, no people in any of the houses he'd robbed. What he did find, in every case, were weird arrangements. Lots of statuary in odd places: a porphyry bust on a kitchen counter, a marble ballerina balanced awkwardly on a couch. Hundreds of photographs. The seventh house had puppets dangling by strings from the ceiling. The sight of that, in semi-darkness, was nearly enough to send Otis out.

Such was his talent for thievery that he could have paid off his debt by the sixth trip. But to his own surprise, and certainly the twins', he did not. Instead he drew from them more credit. Just enough that he could buy something to eat when he was out, instead of relying on the rations Craig provided. Just enough to buy a real beer now and then—even if he had to drink it outside, in the cold, for fear of being questioned.

Anyway, his hauls were good ones, and they pleased the Casey-Feldmans. He knew this because Briony ceased finishing sentences with that sing-y lilt that suggested he was doomed. She'd been particularly tickled by the bedding and towels he'd brought on the second day, which were of a quality that commanded a real price, even outside the Relief Space.

Otis stood in a train car, remembering the way Briony had pressed the towels against her cheek, smiling at their softness with what seemed like genuine pleasure. Commuters were pressing into him on all sides, looking at their tablets or even old print books, Otis feeling nestled in the middle of them, instead of crowded, herded and trapped, as he would have in Annex. This was rush hour. Otis liked to ride at rush hour now.

As usual the other passengers did not interact, or even look up. Otis noticed the businessman among them—the one in the brown suit—standing nearby, head bent over his tablet. He had seen this man several times now.

On the man's display was the abacus-design: the symbols unintelligible to Otis, and probably to most people. This man worked on the same kind of stuff Murray Van Dyck had: financial tools, balance sheets, project costings—all updated and recalibrated by the hour as new information washed in and changed everything.

With each stop the crowd in the train car thinned. By the time it reached Keele there were a handful of riders left, the man in the brown suit among them, filing out of the car in orderly fashion. Otis, being the biggest, went last. With two fingers he hooked the strings of his bag, which had been wedged between his shoes, swung it ahead of him with a certain good cheer and moved to step out. In that moment—a coordination of movements between one foot and the bag, the bag sailing ahead of the foot, headed out through the doorway—the train lurched forward, clearing the end of the Plexiglass shelter. Otis's foot found no purchase, only air, with chain-link fence in front of him and the track below. In shock he grabbed the edge of the doorway, saving his life; the train screeching to a halt again—a brief glitch, instantly righted. But it was enough. His drawstring bag, and with it his lovely copper box, fell onto the track below, sticking deep in the screaming white flow of Optimal Power.

15

"THIS DELAY IS ridiculous; unacceptable." The man in the brown suit punctuated each word by tapping his palm. His name was Evan Carling. This was something Evan did: Evan stood up for people.

Otis stood to one side, watching Evan argue with the transit officer—a stoop-shouldered woman in a green coat who'd joined them in the Keele shelter nearly an hour after he'd lost his bag. Every time another train passed by, Otis winced. Every time Evan tapped his palm the officer nodded.

"This gentleman's property will be returned to him," she said finally. "It fell onto the track from the train, so it's not in a spot any other train can reach." She turned to Otis. "Do you need anything to eat?"

"No."

"We can get you something, probably." She looked him up and down. "A sandwich and some hot coffee."

"I'm fine."

The officer turned back to Evan. "We'll need an address. If he's in one of the Winter Relief Spaces—"

"What does it matter? He's here now. Aren't you going to bring him the bag?"

"I don't have the equipment to do that. We need

to send in a specialized car, with an insulated arm. If I were to climb down there—"

"No one's asking you to risk your life."

"And anyway, he's got to fill out some forms—"

"Oh that's nonsense," Evan said. "I'm with *OP*; Vice-President, Accounting. While you were making this gentleman wait for you, I called my team—to find out if we had any kind of power surge that could've explained what happened. We didn't. Everything's smooth. Which means there's something wrong with this section of track."

"I wouldn't know about that."

"You need to look into it, immediately. And don't worry about forms, because you'll be looking at enough of them yourself over the next few days. Please—just retrieve this man's property ASAP so he can get on with his day." Evan and the officer looked pityingly at Otis, and then the officer left.

"Well, I'd best be getting along too," Evan said, and he shook Otis's hand. "Good luck with this. I'm sure they won't damage anything that was in there."

"Yeah. Look, I appreciate your help—y'know, saying that." Otis had been with Evan the whole time. Evan had never called his team to check anything. "I don't think she much cared what I thought."

"Did you lose anything of value?" Evan asked. All he could see was the bag, sitting maddeningly few feet below them.

"A box with some tools in it. Good tools."

"You're a tradesperson, then? Or you were, before?"

Otis shook his head. "Artificial Personality Calibrator, First Class—fully credentialed." He watched Evan's face. "I was at *Optimal Power* too."

Evan looked awkward. "A while back, I gather?"

"My whole division was let go."

"That would be—"

"Robotics. We kept the android fleet running."

Every company the size of *OP* had a fleet of androids. They assisted with human-mainframe interface. If you integrated them into your workforce, and took care of them, they provided you with a level of market forecasting and predictive HR that no stationary computer could match. But Otis didn't say any of this, because Evan surely knew it.

"I—I really need to go." The businessman headed toward the shelter exit. Otis called after him.

"Do you know Murray?"

"What?"

"Murray Van Dyck. Did you know him?"

Evan paused. "Did he work with you?"

"He was in Accounting. Still there after I left."

"Ah."

"You know him?"

Evan thought about it a moment. "I met Murray, yeah. It's a big department, so I didn't know him well. He got a lot of people fired, Otis—budget cuts and all that. All the smart ones, like you: gone." He continued on his way, calling back, sounding more like his cheerful self: "But he's been gone a long time too!"

16

OTIS SAT UNDER his tree in the Relief Space, his copper box in front of him. The officer had returned it, and the rest of his belongings, with all the speed of someone afraid of Evan Carling.

He'd always suspected that Murray knew about the firing ahead of time. But he never imagined the little twerp had orchestrated it. Not that Murray was incapable of that kind of duplicity—you could smell the man's weakness, his weak character, the rot beneath the thin surface of him. But to be so ruthless to a neighbor, to run the risk of him finding out, someone so close to him—

Otis nudged the box with his foot—

So close to him, physically! Maybe Murray'd had more stones than he thought.

But Murray was stupid. Stupid if he thought that getting rid of Otis and the rest of the division was a smart move. *Optimal Power* was a huge, rich company that owned 200 MAC Total Corporate Management Androids—state of the art models. If even a third of those androids went offline for any length of time, the company's capacity to regulate power distribution and predict market trends could be compromised past the point of recovery. That was why Otis and his colleagues had been so important. They, and they alone, were experts at regulating and mitigating personality shifts, psychosis buildup, and other flaws that crept into any android, no matter how advanced, over time. For androids, just like the human beings they served, could be hobbled by stress. They could be made to feel helpless, undervalued, even victimized. And when that happened, their capacity for risk assessment, trend analysis, would degrade. Since *Optimal Power* was not about to replace its fleet, its Accounting Department had always defended Otis and his colleagues when they'd requested more time, more funds, better equipment. The cost of maintaining these androids, like the gargantuan cost of buying one in the first place, was more than offset by the value they created.

Otis's train of thought was broken by shouting above him. Then rustling in the brush. He clutched the copper box close to his chest, searching for the source of the commotion. There was more arguing, cursing, then the snapping of branches as a pair of young men tumbled down the slope in a whorl of limbs and dirt and leaves, landing at his feet. They recovered and continued battling on the ground.

Otis rose in disgust. Holding the box in one hand, he grabbed the nearer man, then planted a heavy boot on the shoulder of the other one—pulling them apart, roughly, as he might have two dogs. They both sat up, stunned at the sudden parting, and stared at him.

"He took my spot, Otis," said one; red-faced, panting and pointing. "I been there all season!" He pressed his wrist to the side of his head. "You seen where I am. It's that same place."

The other man, bigger and stronger, strained against Otis's grip. "You didn't leave anything there! You didn't leave nobody to hold it," he spat. "I just been laid off—I gotta move here. I got no choice."

"That's not my problem."

"Just 'cause you been here longer, you think you got dibs on the middle—"

"Everybody knows that's my place!"

"So I gotta freeze, then?"

"Stop it!" Otis jerked the near one by his collar and then they were both quiet. "Share it if you have to," he said. "Make do."

The men said nothing. Both of them looked around Otis's space. It was a nice space, big enough for three. Otis glared, and the men cringed.

"I've got enough for me," he said. "That's all anybody should want."

17

SOUTHWEST OF OTIS's old home was Dundas Street West, which ran through the center of the Junction. It was a street made up mostly of commercial properties, with buildings rising no more than three stories and little development further down, so that if you looked far enough, the north and south sides of the street seemed to collect into a mass of red, brown and yellow brick; foliage and road—all of it a base for a vast, unbroken skyscape.

Otis and Angie used to walk along Dundas on weekends. Sometimes they would head to the local diner, splitting a couple of plates; other times they had no destination in mind—just wanting to spend time in the sunshine, in each other's company. When Otis lost his job they began doing this during the week, too. They would window shop, stopping before displays that exemplified good design. Angie said she had an eye for these things, and Otis didn't argue, what with her being an artist, and lately quite an appreciated one.

Since he'd begun his morning commutes, Otis found himself retracing the path he and Angie had taken along Dundas. Yes, this carried a bit of risk, since he was burglarizing the neighborhood, but Otis had never seen so much as a bulletin, in any medium, on any format, calling attention to a threat. And it made him feel good, doing this—like a real citizen. He felt free. He felt like someone who belonged in his city again.

He stopped before a store that he and Angie used to frequent. In those days it had been an appliance store, noted for its brilliant window displays: candy-colored retro-future mixers and blenders and sleek white washing machines and ovens. A quality window display, his wife explained to him one afternoon, allows anyone to see a reflection of themselves. Their potential selves.

People misunderstand that, she went on, her voice betraying the frustration of someone who had to communicate complex concepts to simple people on the regular. They think it means everyone dreams of owning the same things, living the same life. Of course that's not true. No, Otis. Nothing has a single facet. People are sensitive, far more sensitive than we give them credit for. We react to color, shape, value, even texture—but each of us absorbs those aspects differently. What I'm trying to say—and here she'd laced her arm through his—is that bad displays give two people two images that are incompatible, but a good one—like this one!—gives each of them an image that can be reconciled with the other.

He remembered her turning in toward him, warmly. I look at this window and see the ubiquity of beauty, she said. It can be in all things, in mundane things. And if we can have that—a little bit of beauty, a bit of art, in everything—shouldn't we strive for it? She squeezed his arm tighter. But tell me what you see, honey. Otis told her that he saw the harmony of the old and the new: designs from the past informing designs of the future. She'd smiled, and then they'd gone into the store.

But Otis hadn't seen that. He'd only seen the price tags on those appliances; thought only of what they could no longer afford. He couldn't tell Angie this. It was becoming impossible to tell her what he saw and felt—not just in special windows, but in other parts of life—things that, at first, tended to differ just a little from how she saw them, and then almost always did, and by a lot. Soon he was doing most of his walking on Dundas by himself. And usually he was headed to a bar.

This was the same window he and Angie had stood in front of that day. The proprietor was different now—a clothier, not a high-end home appliance retailer. On display now were suits, many of them pricey; fine European styles, suitable, read a sign in one corner, even for the larger man.

Otis considered his reflection in this window. It was a grungy, distorted version of him; an insubstantial image, overlaying the fine clothes inside. This was the look of a man who'd maybe worked a trade; who'd lifted things for a living. A man who needed free coffee and a sandwich. Who lived in a park.

He went into the store.

18

HAD **ANYONE PASSED** the corner of Keele Street and Junction Road that night, they would have seen a broad-shouldered man in a fine top coat, black slacks and shiny boots, engrossed in the display of a fine new Richpainted wooden tablet.

Had they passed close enough, they would have seen a briefcase resting on the sidewalk, braced between the man's shins as he worked. They would have even recognized the webpage he was looking at— if not by the text than by the familiar logo of MOTIV Android Corp. at the top.

However, no one passed that corner—not a single person in the hour Otis stood there, reading MAC Total Corporate Management Android promotional copy on the MOTIV website.

Imagine an android with the mind of a CEO.

Imagine a machine with the capacity to revolutionize your business: Knowledgeable . . . Far-thinking . . . Tireless . . . Adaptable . . . With up-to-date skills you can count on.

This is the MAC Total Corporate Management Android.

The MAC TCMA possesses the data-sets of top AIs

in the fields of Accounting, Resource Extraction, Energy Management, Customer Service and Workforce Management, supplementing it with intuition, empathy and relatability that no non-humanoid computer can provide. The TCMA learns how you think—so it can think the same way. There is no more efficient, effective way to stop Function Drift in your company.

Available in multiple body types for seamless integration.

At the end of the page was an ordering link.

Otis scrolled through other pages: product reviews; forums; op-eds; corporate analyses. 'Best value'; he read. 'Remarkably effective and fast'; 'A necessity for any company serious about heavy crunching'; 'Say goodbye to your android therapists!'

That last one stung.

Optimal Power had indeed said goodbye to its android therapists, apparently with no ill effects. But Otis knew those androids weren't flawless. They'd needed people like him. They would always need people like him.

He closed the display.

He remained on the corner, looking at his old home, sealed and silent.

19

GEORGIA AND FELICITY jostled each other for a closer look at Otis's tablet. He'd placed it on the grass for them, under the shade of his tree, while he sat nearby, the copper box open on his lap, gazing at the tools inside. The tools glinted as brightly as the box did: each pick and prod, hook and scraper fashioned for a particular, delicate task, to be executed only by the most skillful hands. Otis smiled. Each tool was, itself, the product of delicate craftsmanship.

"D'you mind if we play *Crush Farm,* Otis?"

"Be my guests, girls." Otis closed the box and tucked it back into his drawstring bag, hearing it clink against the pistol. He stuffed the whole bag into his briefcase and shut the case quickly. "Just don't get too curious."

The girls brought up the game and spent a few minutes patting pastel-colored animals back and forth. Georgia lost interest first. She turned to Otis.

"What's it like out there?"

"You know what it's like. You go out every summer."

"People are saying it's different now."

"Different how?"

"Different 'cause they can't go everywhere they used to."

"That's true."

"But you can, and now you got all this stuff." She pointed to his clothes; to the briefcase, sitting on the grass; to a long stick of French bread propped against the tree. "People are talking about you," she said.

"What are they saying?"

"They see you dressed nice. They see this stuff. They talk about how you got it."

"Do they have any theories?"

Georgia looked at him fixedly. Her friend was engrossed in the game and wasn't hearing any of this.

"Not me personally," she said. "But other people say you're a thief for the Casey-Feldmans."

"That's not true."

The girl shifted position on the lawn; she looked back at Felicity playing her game. Felicity was wide-eyed, grinning at the painted board.

"I could keep your secrets, Otis," Georgia said. "You can trust me—I know things about lots of people and I never tell."

"What secrets would I have to tell, Georgia?"

"Just—whatever." Georgia picked at the grass. "Like, if I wanted to get something from the outside. Maybe you could get it for me, and I wouldn't tell anybody how I got it."

Otis smiled. "You want one of these tablets."

"No," Georgia said. "I don't care about games. Felicity likes them. I want some blankets."

"What do you need blankets for?"

"You're away so much. You haven't heard." She pointed to the vast discs on the Relief Space's western side. "They're shutting down One and Two next week."

"What?"

"I'm not sure what we'll do," Georgia said, sounding frightened. "If you shut those discs down while people are still here, then they'll have to move inward, but there's already people everywhere—"

"Has anyone talked to Craig?"

"Craig says *OP*'s calling in its debts. The government can't do anything. They can't pay. Craig says the company's acting strange. Otis—" Georgia glanced at Felicity, whose head stayed lowered over the game.

"—will you get us some blankets?"

20

THE SKY WAS dark by five o'clock that night. Liandre Damerle nudged her business partner, Michael Largo, with her elbow. Pointed to the man sitting at a little table by the window, looking out onto Dundas Street.

"Who is that?" she asked, stacking three slices of banana bread onto a plate.

"He's come in a few times now. Usually later in the day." Michael was working the espresso machine, cleaning the head of the steam wand with a rag. "You were away."

"I wish I hadn't been."

Michael laughed. Half the fun of owning a café, Liandre had told him, was the people-watching. He handed her a latte, for table three. "Do you think he's that good looking?" he asked. "I mean, he's big, if you like that."

"Not good looking," Liandre said. "Just familiar."

Otis was sitting low in his chair, resting his foot on the base of the café's bay window, a coffee cup half-full on his lap. He would hit one of the biggest houses tonight: a near-mansion, with a pair of superfluous

Roman columns and a turret built into the rooftop—a house designed to excess, certainly stuffed with valuable junk. That job was hours away yet. Outside the weather looked gentle, a few flakes of snow meandering their way to the ground. But it was cold.

This had been their diner once. Back then it had booths with red vinyl cushions and a bar with circular stools. The bar remained, but wood accents had replaced the chrome; oak armchairs and loveseats had replaced the booths. The lighting was softer.

It made him a little drowsy, actually.

He loosened the collar of his new shirt, a long-sleeved, 100% cotton dress shirt, dark-green and shiny, that the sales clerk assured him would draw attention. Otis had bought it anyway. Behind the bar the two staffers—he gathered they owned the place, but he wasn't sure—were jawing. Maybe about him.

Otis positioned his briefcase upright on the table, forming a barrier. He touched his tablet, spots of energy forming above it, coalescing into a news page on the federal government's website. The site was choked with pop-ups, as government websites tended to be, Otis's hand clenching in irritation, bouncing on his knee as he tried to read it.

The Canadian government's position on the contraction of the Annex Winter Relief Space—and more than three-hundred other Relief Spaces across the country—was to blame *OP*. The company, the government claimed, had abruptly ceased negotiations, demanding an immediate 75-percent repayment of the government's debt. The company must have known this was impossible. In a statement dated three days before, Prime Minister Barbara Carnaffan expressed regret and anger at this new, hardline stance:

"It has been more than a year since executives at *OP* last met with any representative of our government," she said. "This government has long supported *OP*'s operations in Canada, which is why we awarded them the exclusive contract to power Winter Relief Spaces in fifteen of our large cities. And yet *OP* continues to demand more—continues to squeeze the most vulnerable in our society. Every one of these Relief Spaces is full to capacity. This policy change, made only days ago—again, without any kind of public announcement, or even advance warning to this government or anyone else—puts the lives of hundreds of thousands of people—"

"Top up?"

The female staffer was standing over Otis with an urn. He swiped his display shut; nudged his briefcase to one side.

"Sure."

She filled his mug. "Need anything else?" she asked politely.

"Um, not yet. I'll get something else in a bit."

"So you're gonna be here a while?"

"I'd planned to be. Is that a problem?"

"Not at all." The woman sat down in the seat opposite Otis. She produced a second mug from the pocket of her apron and filled it for herself.

"I have spent an hour," she said quietly, "trying to remember who you are."

Otis removed his tablet from the table.

"My name's Liandre," the woman said. "I'm one of the owners. But I worked here before. I waited tables. How about you?"

"You mean, where did I work?"

"I mean, did you used to come to the diner?"

"Yes. With my wife."

"Who's your wife?"

"My ex-wife. She's an artist—"

Liandre pointed at him and grinned. "That's it," she said. "You were Angie Shomar's husband."

Otis nodded, looking out the window.

"You and her used to come in here together, I remember now. You'd always split two plates—one all greens and fruit, the other greasy. You went halfsies."

"That was a long time ago."

"Not really though, right?" Liandre rested her chin in one hand and looked at him, sideways. "We talk like that, don't we?— about how 'long ago' things were. When they weren't. The other day I was telling Michael—" she motioned her mug toward the bar, "—about this guy I'd been dating, and how I missed him, you know, just a bit, after all this time, and he says, 'Liandre, you guys split up like three months ago!' I was talking like it'd been three, four years." She sipped her coffee. "I used to say time flies. But maybe it's us that go too fast now? Like, so much stuff happens all at once, so we act like it's happening over a longer time. That's the only way we can comprehend it."

Otis shrugged.

"Yeah, that's what I think," Liandre said.

The snow was falling heavier now. Otis watched the people outside, their hats and coats whitening as they trudged along. The waitress tapped the side of his briefcase and he returned to attention.

"So what do you do?" she asked.

"Nothing much."

"Nice briefcase though." She traced its surface with her fingernail. "Did you used to do something?"

"I worked for *Optimal Power*."

"*OP*?"

"Sure, whatever they call it now. I worked there before."

"Doing what?"

Otis paused. He supposed he should be more circumspect. Just stop talking. Get up and leave right now. But his coffee wasn't finished. And it was cold outside, and here, inside, was a woman who wanted to talk to him.

"I was an Artificial Personality Calibrator, First Class, fully credentialed—like an android therapist," he replied. "When any of the androids in *OP*'s fleet started to get weird, one of us was called in to recalibrate it."

"The androids got weird when you were there?"

He straightened in his chair.

"Androids are always at work. They don't have homes or lives, just work. They wear out fast, and as they do, the parts that are still functioning begin to compensate. It's the means by which they compensate: the patterns, the workarounds, whatever you call it, that they come up with, that cause the problems. Because nobody can predict exactly how the androids'll form those workarounds—what they'll fixate on; prioritize. And since the reason *OP*, or any company, purchases an android fleet is because of the precision of its processing power, it's not a great thing when the androids become unpredictable."

"No, no—it definitely isn't," Liandre said. "But you fixed that?"

"Yeah, I can. I have the skills and the tools, too. And I have—I guess you could call it faith, in those machines. In their capabilities." Otis took a quick sip of his coffee. "An android, when it's new, it'll find answers to any question you put to it. But as the damage starts to build up, they start answering your questions with questions of their own. They stop trusting the explanations you give them. They've been hurt, and they're trying to avoid more hurt. That almost sounds like cynicism, doesn't it?"

Otis paused, until Liandre realized she was supposed to nod. He went on.

"We used to debate whether it was cynicism—Monica, my colleague, she said it was; but Ronda said it was anthropomorphism to call it that. Cynicism is what we'd call it, but it's not cynicism, she said. It's an android's approximation of cynicism. Maybe a simulation of cynicism. I agree—I agreed, I mean—with Ronda. We didn't make these machines to be like us. When they break down, get weird, they haven't 'changed' the way a human being changes. They just need to be fixed." Otis felt sheepish all of a sudden; overcaffeinated. "Anyway, these were the sorts of debates we had all the time. What we all agreed on was that it didn't matter how state-of-the-art MOTIV's models were, what innovative hardware or software they contained—the weirdness always kicked in. So we always had something to do. We were all needed."

Liandre whistled.

"Wow," she said, filling her mug again. She motioned the urn toward Otis, who declined.

"So," she said, "I work there."

She caught his surprised look.

"That's not strange, is it? Running a place like this, in times like these, well, it's good to have something on the side. Another gig. I've been a receptionist there for almost a year. Never saw you there."

"I've been gone longer than that."

"Which would explain it." Liandre turned her attention back to the briefcase. To the scuffing already visible on its underside.

"How are things in the Relief Spaces?" she asked. "I've been wondering."

"Not great. The government owes *OP* a lot of money. *OP*'s shutting off the heat to make up for it. There's going to be a crisis."

"People'll freeze, then?"

"Or get sick. Or crowd together and get hurt."

Liandre rested her fingers on the top of her mug, rotating it slowly on the table top. "I don't know why *OP*'s doing this."

"Nobody does."

"It's been nonstop meetings at Headquarters, for the last two weeks. Had to tell them, flat out, that I was working here tonight. It's not like they really need me. I think the only reason I got hired was because there was an opening when the other girl quit. And no one—I mean, there was nobody left to say, 'just get rid of that position.'"

"That's strange."

"It's weird, you mean." Liandre took a long drink of her cooling coffee, peering over the mug at Otis. "You should visit *OP*."

"I'm not allowed."

"I wish you were. I'd like your expert opinion. I'd like somebody to tell me what's going on at *OP*, and why." She sighed. "And I'd love somebody to talk to."

"Me too." As Otis said this he felt the guardedness slipping out of him. It wasn't a relaxation of discipline, just an easing of bodily tension. The table felt warm and safe. As though he and Liandre were home together.

"I'll tell you everything I know," she said, "if you promise to visit *OP*."

Otis promised to try, and she began.

21

HE LEFT THE café an hour later, full of new information—skipping the planned job and heading straight for his old home. The second-floor window was lit. Otis pulled his shoulders back, gripped his suitcase handle tightly, and knocked on the front door.

The light winked out overhead. But no one opened up.

Behind him shone National Headquarters, bright against the night sky. Framed, as Angie had long ago intended it, between the branches of two trees she'd had transplanted to the hillside. The black outlines of their trunks—one thick and squat, the other slender, wispy—appeared to stand on either side of the tower: the gnarled claws of one tree mingling with the fine fingers of the other, making a mesh of black that the tower's sick light pulsed through.

Otis locked eyes on that building. He reached back, brushing his fingers against the doorknob—just a casual, non-committal touch. The lock gave way for him, as all locks did, and he leaned against the door, and it drifted open.

The house was dark, but Otis knew, from the broad shapes of the objects ahead of him—almost from the flow of air around him—that this was much the same room he'd walked out of five years ago. He looked past the sitting area, to the opening that led to the kitchen. That spot: she'd stood in that spot the last time he'd seen her, one hand gripping her waist, the other covering her eye—holding in her humiliation, the last of her rage; her whole body seeming to swirl and sway through his inebriated gaze. He'd opened his mouth to say something—he couldn't remember what, maybe an apology, maybe an excuse, and what came out had been a garbled mess. He'd pivoted out of the doorway, onto the stoop, and the door slammed shut behind him. He could not open it again. Not even one second later.

Everything that belonged to him had stayed here, except for the copper box. She'd given it to him, through her lawyer, the lawyer asking Otis, on Angie's behalf, if he would take anything else: photos, mementos, things that had been his before they met. Otis said no, and the lawyer pressed him, asking one final time, because, he said, this was a decision he suspected Otis would regret. Otis repeated himself: no.

No, nothing but the copper box.

There was someone standing in the opening. Not a statue, just someone quiet, waiting for him to stay something.

"I'm not a thief," Otis called out. He was surprised by the weakness of his voice. "I'm not going to hurt you."

"Then why are you here?" the figure asked.

"To talk. Just to talk. Is this your house?"

"Unofficially." The room snapped into brightness. Evan Carling walked in, sat down, holding a tumbler of whiskey in one hand. He was in sock feet. "It's you, isn't it, Otis?" he asked, directing Otis to a rocking chair in front of him. "You're the one pilfering things from the houses around here."

Otis said nothing.

"Yeah; yeah it's you. It's you." Evan gulped from the glass, then set it on a side table, gently, without finding a coaster—keeping his hand on it as he continued. "You're here to talk. About how things are, I guess. About why. I'd be the one to ask."

"That's what I was hoping, Mr. Carling."

"Oh Jesus, call me Evan. At least do that." He returned the glass to his lap. "I'm not an employee at *OP*, Otis. I never was. But I do some work for them, offsite. I used to be a curator at an art gallery downtown—I handled purchases. Now I do that for *OP*. They own most of the houses around here now. They told me I could stay in one. I thought it'd be nice to stay in an artist's house, y'know?"

"So you're boarding."

"I'm staying out of a Relief Space, is what I'm doing. This whole area's bogged, Otis. I can get around because I have an exemption, you might call it—I have knowledge that's useful to the company. They want my advice. They need it. Things are—well, they're not as sharp as they used to be, over there." He pointed toward the front door. "And you can get around, I guess, because you're some kind of burglar."

"I met a woman tonight, who works there."

"Liandre."

"She told me what's going on."

"Maybe. There's a lot Liandre knows, and a lot she

doesn't know. There are things only I know. The question is what you know. What you've figured out."

"I know why the company's the way it is."

"Okay. That's fine, I guess."

"And I know that I'm to blame for what it's doing."

"That's better." Evan sunk back in his chair. "Those poor people in the Relief Spaces, Otis: you've got to make things right."

"I have a plan. I'm hoping it'll work. Otherwise—"

"Otherwise what?"

"I'll have to kill somebody."

"Have you ever done that before?"

"I don't know. I've defended myself, when I had to, and I didn't always stick around to make sure the other guy was alright."

Evan considered Otis's frame. "I can imagine someone not being alright. Yeah, yeah I can." The ice in his glass sat piled above the liquid. "You fix this, you'll be defending yourself. And not just yourself. Think of it that way."

Otis thought of Georgia and Felicity.

"I've got a gun," he said. "If I have to, I'll use my gun."

22

THE FOLLOWING AFTERNOON, without Otis's shiny new tablet to distract them, Georgia and Felicity returned to their guessing game.

Georgia dropped the dice on the pavement. "It's a nine," she said.

Felicity didn't say anything.

"It's a nine," Georgia repeated. "Felicity—"

"I know."

"No. You didn't—know." Georgia felt foolish, suddenly. "You didn't predict it right. You said it would be five."

"I'm kind of preoccupied." Felicity crossed her legs on the grass and sniffed the air. She began rubbing her arms. "Something's wrong."

"Craig said they wouldn't be shutting off any discs except One and Two—for now," Georgia said. She thought it best to comfort her friend, though she didn't understand what had come over her so suddenly. Felicity was rarely this grave. "Anyway, we've got a few more days to worry about it."

"It's not phantom cold that's bothering me," Felicity murmured. "Have you seen Otis today?"

"Early this morning."

"When—" Felicity seemed headachy; she closed

her eyes. "D'you know if he's getting the blankets soon? Did he already get them?"

"I don't think so. He never said he'd buy us blankets though, right? Or steal them, I guess. He never promised."

"But we need those blankets! We need something! We can't live in here if everybody's pushed together. Did you hear what happened last night? Down by the bathing pool—"

"That wouldn't happen to us, Felicity. Those girls were stupid to go there so late."

"It will happen to us! If we don't get out of here!"

Georgia picked up the dice, jangling them in her hand a moment. She stuffed them in her pocket and stood up, brushing dirt off the seat of her shorts. She took Felicity by the shoulders and drew her up, in close, and spoke to her:

"I talked to him again this morning. He said he'd 'fix things.' He'd fix the problem."

"How? How could any one person do that? Georgia—"

"He said he had the answer. He knew how to fix everything."

Felicity pulled back. "I wish he'd just brought us blankets," she said. "I wish he'd done it yesterday."

23

BRIONY STOOD FACE to face with Otis and gave him a sniff.

"You, sir, have cleaned up well." She circled him to confirm it. "The more I see, the more I like. Even if it does back up your debt a bit!"

Otis kept his attention on Benny, who remained perched on the upholstery-throne a few yards away. Benny looked tired and irritable. "It's backing it up a lot," he called out. "You've got expensive tastes, Otis."

"You're getting quality goods from me."

"And if you slip up?" Benny flicked a finger toward Otis's latest ensemble. "If you get pinched in one of these houses? We don't get our money back. Then word'll get around that we let your debt drag out—let it slide. That you got away with it."

"By going to prison?"

"You'd choose prison over what we'd do to you."

Briony stayed close. "Benny does have a point, doesn't he? About us looking soft."

"I can pay off the suit—and then some—in one night," Otis said quietly, just to Briony. "I know just the place to hit." Now he projected, so Benny could hear him: "I'm here to negotiate!"

"Negotiate?" Benny leaned perilously far forward.

"Negotiate what? You owe us money, Otis. The only point of discussion is how soon we're getting it."

"You'll get all your money tonight if you expand my access. Get me into *Optimal Power*'s Headquarters."

Benny had a response for that too. But Briony held up her hand and her brother stayed silent.

"You're planning to rob *OP*?" she asked.

Otis nodded. "They've got a world-class art collection. I could walk out with 300 grand in one night. You're gonna need that. The people in here who owe you money: a lot of them are going to disappear, or die, when those discs shut off. Get me access to that tower and you'll be in the black for the rest of the year."

It was a fair proposition. One that spoke to the Casey-Feldmans' greed: the prime mover in their lives. Otis watched Benny, puny emperor that he was, mulling it over from atop his throne. Every twitch of that pinched little face, he thought, could mark disaster. But it was Briony, not Benny, who spoke first.

"Otis, you're just—you're just so black and white about everything." She patted his hand. "Some people will pull in, or fade away, but not before we get what's coming to us."

"Believe it or not, we are willing to forgive some debts!" Benny said. "Y'know: for those poor souls just as deep in debt as you, but without your singular intelligence and moral fortitude." He smirked and gestured past Otis, to a mass of men gathering among the planters. Towering over them was the Casey-Feldmans' guard.

"Annex thins out every spring," Briony said.

"We've always kept a small retinue of men to help us settle debts before that happens. This year things are less certain, less predictable. And so—" she twirled her hand in the air—"—if some deadbeat gets it in their head, even after seeing all our loyal soldiers amassed this way, to take their chances on the outside, well, I promise you that any of these men will happily assist us with collection."

"Imagine," Benny called out. "Getting your whole debt wiped out in a single day. Just by busting a few heads."

There had to be forty men behind Otis. Thin, hungry men, clustered together in the aisleways between the planters. He found the planter nearest him and pressed his back against it.

"I need access to *OP*!"

"Pay off your debt!" Benny snapped. "Then I'll think about it."

The men were close enough to be heard. They were desperate, fearful; murmuring to one another, too low to be intelligible. Benny kept talking. "I mean, who do you think you are? Trying to dictate terms to us? It's always been this way with you, Otis: you think you're a special case. You think you're better than us. You think you're better than those people behind you! You, with your—your—shiny suit."

"I'll give you the suit!"

"I don't want your fucking suit, Otis!"

Benny leaned back on his cushions, resting his head on one hand. "All this time, you've been using our money to turn yourself back into what you used to be. Right? Suit, shoes, shirts, briefcase—like you're some big-deal business guy instead of a bum. But you're still a bum, Otis. Take all that fancy stuff off and people see it. They see what's inside. Now, I don't have any use for your shoes, or shirts or even your suit—you're such a giant fucking freak, they wouldn't fit anybody else. But I am interested in that briefcase."

"You can have the briefcase."

"I mean what's in it. That briefcase never leaves your side, Otis; you won't even leave it at the Barn, so whatever's in there must be real valuable. If you want another loan—if you want this access you're asking us for—then give us what's inside."

For a moment Otis was lost. He stared at Briony, hoping she might interject—redirect the course of events, which seemed to him certain now, and terrifying. But Briony's response was nothing. She was, after all, just the cordial side of her brother, another facet of the same cheap stone.

He rested his briefcase on the ground, kneeling slowly in front of it. Unlocked it—conscious of his movements, trying his best to appear non-threatening, as he had that night when the statue looked down on him from the stairs. He removed the copper box from the briefcase, then closed the case.

"This is a set of tools," he said. "Tools of the highest quality."

The twins squinted—two pairs of eyes, mean and calculating, resting on Otis's prize. He opened the box for them, the tools sparkling inside; Briony giving the high-sign to the guard, who came forward from the crowd and snatched it out of Otis's hands. Otis did not see the guard coming; he rubbed his palm where the edge of the metal scraped it, watching the guard pass Briony and deliver the box to her brother.

"They'll go for a lot," Briony said, keeping her eyes

on Otis. Benny was holding the box in front of his face; picking at one of the clasps with his thumbnail.

"I dunno," he said, turning it over. "Bottom's scuffed."

"It's not scuffed."

"He says it's not scuffed, Benny."

Benny made an exaggerated shrug. He looked down at the guard, who remained by the upholstery throne. "What do you think, Greg? Is it shiny enough?"

"Just tell me when you can give me access."

"It'll just take a few minutes," Briony said. "The hack's previously established, and it hasn't been compromised, so—you could wait."

"By all means Otis, stick around!" Benny added. "It's not like you've got anything better to do!"

24

"C'MON, C'MON!"
Georgia squealed as Felicity pulled her by the wrist, odors of filth and sweat surrounding them as they forced their way through a press of bigger bodies. Georgia elbowed a large woman, who elbowed her back; sending her toward the railing of the causeway.

The girls shimmied along the railing, keeping their skinny backs to the crowd.

"Down there, see?" Felicity said, cocking her head. Georgia looked down and saw what Felicity saw: a steady flow of bodies, heading toward the Casey-Feldmans' base of operations. They observed the crowd from above as best they could; keeping to the railing, stepping around other people who'd begun to notice the crowd too, and were stopping to watch. The girls reached the end of the causeway, looking further east. Georgia couldn't see Otis anywhere. "We could get closer. We could get down, and get closer."

Felicity shook her head. The crowd below kept growing, filling the spaces between the planters, mixing in among the forty men in the Casey-Feldmans' employ, but no one ventured past them. From up here they could just make out the siblings' colorful upholstery throne.

"D'you see him now?" Georgia whispered.

Felicity put her hands on either side of Georgia's head and gently moved it to the left. Then she pointed toward a planter in the row closest to the throne. She bobbed her finger, like she was keeping time.

Georgia swallowed.

Five, six, seven times the finger bobbed. And then Otis's head appeared above the planter, and Felicity closed her fingers and buried her head in Georgia's shoulder. "I don't wanna watch," she said. "I don't wanna see what's coming."

Otis crouched against the planter, his suit jacket folded on his thigh. He'd grown warm in the jacket as he waited for Benny to complete the access request—the heat making him sweat, plastering his shirt against his back. Reddening his face, like he'd been laboring hours in the sun, rather than cutting a deal in the highest of high-pressure situations. He could hear the growing crowd behind him—just curiosity seekers, he hoped, rather than more of the twins' recruits—but he didn't turn to look. He couldn't spare a thought for them now.

Otis had to get those tools back.

A few yards away, atop the upholstery throne, Benny was flicking at icons. He held Otis's copper box in his other hand, tapping it absently against the side of his head as he worked. He seemed not to be in any hurry.

"How much longer, Benny?" called out Briony, who remained near Otis.

Benny didn't reply.

Otis opened his briefcase again. Drew out a strip

of cloth and dabbed his brow with it. "How much longer?" he called out. "C'mon!"

Benny glared at him. "You're just one more dumb thug," he said, setting a hologram spinning with one finger. Briony turned to her brother. Otis couldn't see her face, but it seemed like a long moment.

"I don't think he's going to do it," Otis whispered, just to her.

"You gave us the box, so we'll give you access. That was the deal."

"Ask him what the hold-up is."

"It won't make any difference. He's taking his time, because it's you."

Benny was balancing the copper box on one end, with two fingers. Otis watched him shift his small body around on the cushions, trying to keep the box level. Benny was having fun.

"Tell him to hurry up!"

"I don't take orders from you, buster! Neither does he."

The box made wobbly pirouettes on Benny's fingers. He didn't care if the box fell, it seemed like—those tools inside were delicate, didn't he realize how delicate they were? If they hit the ground, from that height—even if the box stayed shut, they could break. Otis needed those tools. He needed every one of them.

"My brother's very distractable," Briony piped in. "Give him a minute, he'll get back to work."

The box teetered—the boy twin extending his arm slowly, carefully, outward from the throne, the box tipping a little more, further from safety—

Otis cursed; loud enough to get Briony's attention. He opened the briefcase again, tugging out the drawstring bag. "What's in there?" she asked. "Another tool?"

Briony jumped as she saw him pull out a handgun. Otis glared at her, his face suddenly cruel.

"What do you think of it?" he asked, loudly.

Briony's hands lighted on her hips. Her brother flinched, the copper box falling; landing in the arms of the Casey-Feldmans' guard. Benny rose from his seat, just a little. "You gonna tell me that thing's loaded?" he croaked. His voice lacked its usual conceit.

Otis shook his head. "Not gonna tell you—" he jerked the gun to one side, then the other; a pair of poor wretches withdrawing behind the planter again, back to where they'd been standing. He waited for more movement, but no one came.

Briony glanced at her brother, who was returning, slowly, to his seat. "Otis!" she said, forcing geniality, "where'd you get a pistol? They're so hard to find."

Otis returned to his crouch.

"Survival stuff," he said.

Briony nodded. "Will you sell it too? It's worth more than that box." She tented her fingers in front of her, trying to keep her hands from shaking. "Or— do you plan to wipe out everybody's debt, right now?"

"Like some kind of hero," Benny hissed.

"Get back to work!" Otis cried. And to Briony: "Get me the box. Give it back to me. Now."

Briony hurried to the upholstery throne. She took the copper box from the guard, brought it back to Otis, then resumed her place between them. She could have stayed by her brother and perhaps sped up his work, but she didn't.

Because I didn't tell her she could, Otis thought suddenly, as he tucked the box back into the briefcase and shut it again. "You were never afraid of me before," he murmured.

"I didn't think you were like this," she replied.

I'm not, Otis thought. But he didn't bother saying it.

He could hear the buzz of dozens more voices behind him now, among the planters and further back. They weren't just debtors, they couldn't possibly all be debtors. The tension among them was growing, their numbers building even as they feared to advance. Otis knew they could hear everything.

"You're taking forever, Benny!" he yelled. "How stupid are you?"

Benny kept his head down, fumbling with the icons on his tablet.

"Why's anyone scared of you anyway?" Otis stood now, his head above the planter. He looked behind him, stunned to see a crowd much larger than he'd imagined. "He's not the one you're afraid of, is he?" he called to the people. No one spoke back. They regarded him with a mixture of confusion and awe.

"There isn't a man here who couldn't beat the piss out of Benny Casey-Feldman!"

Briony gathered the fabric of her slacks, squeezing it.

"There isn't a woman who couldn't!"

Please stop, Briony mouthed to him. But Otis did not stop.

"Give me what I want right now—you piece of shit!" he roared. "Or I'm just going to take it!"

Benny's fingers disappeared into the cushions.

"Benny!—" his sister cried.

There was commotion behind Otis, but he ignored it. Briony covered her face, ducking as Otis squeezed the trigger seven times, fast as he could—

—Benny's head flung to one side. His body jerked backward, the tablet flying out of his hands, his legs bouncing straight up as he folded and sunk into the cushions. Below him the guard's legs buckled, his huge body sagging and crashing into the throne; the whole throne collapsing back upon him in a comical heap, burying the guard and Benny both. Otis completed a slow revolution, his gun raised, backing down a trifecta of experienced henchmen that appeared from the crowd.

Briony screamed. But she did not move. "Finish the job!" Otis wheezed, his heart pounding so strongly it blurred his vision. He lurched forward, stepping on his suit jacket, grinding it in the dirt. He passed the terrified woman on his way to her dead brother. Picked up Benny's tablet and threw it at her.

"Finish it! Finish the job!"

25

ONE OF BENNY'S legs was sticking out from the pile. His shoe—it was a slip-on really, almost a slipper, Otis thought wildly—dangled from his big toe. The shoe, the foot, most of the man's shin were exposed, the fabric from his slacks having fallen into the depths of the cushions. The cushions shifted and sagged beneath Otis as he crawled toward the middle of the collapsed throne, the butt of the gun sinking in. Behind him the crowd stayed put—he didn't have to look, he just knew it. Were he one of them, he'd stay put too. To see what happened next.

He reached the middle of the pile, whacking the shoe off Benny's foot with the pistol, flinging the cushions aside till he exposed the body. The sight of it was pathetic. Crumpled and bloody.

You're just one more dumb thug.

Otis sniffed. He would not soil good clothes for the likes of Benny Casey-Feldman.

He rested the gun on a throw-pillow and began unbuttoning his shirt. He was shaking; it was so bad that he couldn't manage the buttons, and so he tugged at them, just a little, but so powerful were Otis's hands that the threads broke, one by one, and in seconds the shirt fell, sodden with sweat, from his shoulders and he was sitting bare chested under the thin winter sun. Briony was still working. Finishing the job.

Otis steadied himself against the shifting cushions. He bent forward, pushing deep as he could into the hole; nudging Benny's ruined corpse out of the way as he dug. Beneath the body, he knew, was the Casey-Feldmans' bin of goods.

When he rose again he had all the things he wanted. He placed one knee on the edge of the opening and pulled himself out, facing the crowd. Facing Briony too. Every one of them beheld him the same way: the great brute, skin slick, smeared with red. Arms full of clothing, the copper box, and some stolen art.

The people followed him out of Town Hall Square, massed as one—their backs turned to Briony Casey-Feldman and the dregs of her brother and throne; the heavies and the hires weaving in with the still-pure victims of circumstance, happy to be forgotten. As they neared the easternmost disc the onlookers up on its deck began to move too, Georgia and Felicity fighting to be in the vanguard, aided by their skinniness, the girls managing to be among the first back down to the ground. They ran toward Otis, the sweating, bloodsmeared hulk that was their friend, caught up to him, touched his bare arms, as dozens of others were trying to do, trying to get his attention.

"Otis!" Felicity cried. "Slow down, Otis!"

"Slow down," said Georgia.

They did not know where he was going, only that he was marching toward the center of Annex. Behind them people called him a hero, or a psychopath; a restorer, a destabilizer. They feared him now, even if they loved what he'd done. Otis did not turn to them, or even slow down, and this apparent indifference made him seem, to them, even more powerful.

"What about our blankets?" Felicity asked. And then he halted.

Otis turned to the girls—toward the whole crowd, really, though only the girls failed to shrink from him. His face was red with fury, his chest still heaving. He thrust one big arm toward Georgia and Felicity; the girls stood dumb before him, then woke up. Drew, from under his arm, two parkas, long and gray, with fur-lined hoods.

The girls clutched their new coats like the treasures they were.

"Thanks Otis," said Georgia.

Otis sniffed. "You're welcome," he said, quietly.

And then to everyone: "I'm leaving. I'm getting the rest of my things from the Barn, and then I'm out of here. I'm going to fix this. One and Two aren't going to go down."

"How are you going to do that?" they asked.

"I'm going to make my case to *Optimal Power*," Otis said. "To the ones who make the decisions." And though this was barely an answer at all, they trusted him—all of them did. Because who could imagine that a man like this, having done the things he'd just done, could fail?

26

SOUTH OF JUNCTION ROAD, well past the white stone wall, was an iron bridge, more than a century old. The bridge was a pathway for freight-bearing vehicles headed to *OP*, but an enclosed staircase, carved into the rock at the base of it, gave pedestrians access to it too.

Otis reached the top of the stairs, crossing along the bridge's center line, the company's courtyard ahead of him. He passed two of the great generators, each the height of an office building and the girth of three city blocks, his big body reduced to that of an insect's before them. The tower was narrower than the generators but taller by half, casting its seafoam-colored hue all around—Otis followed its gentle curve until he came to an entranceway, made of opaque glass. Past this entrance was the lobby, floored with shining marble and accented with chrome and brass, with a big wooden information desk in the center. The lobby had been a busy place when Otis worked here, full of people milling around, doing their business. But as the glass doors parted and Otis stepped inside, he found the room not as he'd remembered it.

It was full, but not with people. It looked, instead, like a cluttered attic.

CHRIS EDWARDS

The lobby was filled with statues. Replicas of the Classic masters' work, and modern ones too: Moore, Duchamp-Villon, Archipenko and others. Otis knew these names, these forms, because of Angie's tutoring, ticking off names and styles and periods as he made his way toward the elevators at the far end of the floor. The statues were arranged in a haphazard and awkward way, as if to prevent visitors from walking in a straight line. Otis recalled the sculpture of the woman and child he'd found on the staircase during his second robbery. That one, too, had obstructed him.

Though the statues varied in style and taste and degree of abstraction they were all concerned with the human form. Otis passed dozens of faces: lifelike evocations, light approximations; faces twisted into every emotion. Bodies, big or small, broad or lean, their limbs laboring or free. He felt, as he worked his way through the crowd of them, that he was setting eyes upon every facet of the human experience. It was only when he neared the elevators that he come across statues he couldn't recognize. These ones were cast exclusively in metals and plastics: their limbs not always whole, but sometimes broken and jagged, sometimes made of several disparate pieces welded together. The figures stood in odd ways: hunched and buckling as though they carried a great burden, yet alien in the manner in which they carried it, as though the burden were universal but the particulars of their anatomies, being different, had failed differently. At first Otis found these sculptures unreadable, but then he did not feel this way. He looked closely at the materials; at their coloring. He found familiar lines and suture-points. The art became aggrieved and wondrous, and he was filled with pity for its creators.

The elevator sent him to the top floor, as he requested. It opened before an old reception desk. Liandre sat at the desk, looking up at him from her tablet.

"That was quick," she said. "How can I help you?"

"I'm honestly not sure."

"I think you're here for the meeting." She gestured toward the boardroom doors on her right. "It's been going on for six days, but I doubt you've missed much."

27

HE'D BEEN IN this boardroom a few times—when there was trouble with the androids, or the likelihood that trouble was coming, he'd ask to come. He would stand before his bosses, a dozen or so of them seated at a long gleaming table, and patiently explain what needed to be done. They would thank him—always a bit amused, he thought, that a man that looked like him knew what he knew, and sounded the way he did. Then he would be dismissed.

The boardroom had not changed. It was still wide and circular, with the long table down the middle. But there were no people in the room now. Only androids. Otis counted more than fifty, seated at the table and all around it, crowding the space; none of them moving. None made any noise. His arrival elicited no reaction from any of them.

"Good day. My name is Otis Colip. I am 47 years of age, single. I identify male. I am currently a resident of the Annex Winter Relief Space.

"I am formerly a resident of 1 Junction Road, where I lived with my wife, prior to our divorce.

"I am formerly an employee of *OP*, then known as *Optimal Power*, where I worked as an Artificial

Personality Calibrator, First Class, fully credentialed. Do any of you remember me?"

The androids remained silent.

"Currently, I am a thief."

He set the briefcase on the table and opened it.

"I've come to you tonight to discuss two subjects of importance to *OP*. Subject One: The contraction of the Winter Relief Spaces. Subject Two: *OP*'s position in the Canadian energy market. May I proceed?"

A small android, sculpted with feminine aspects, sat at the back of the table. She replied to him in a high, dispassionate voice:

"We will allow you 17 hours to make your presentation."

"Thank you," Otis said. "The contraction of the Winter Relief Spaces, prior to the end of the season, puts their residents in harm's way. They will be forced out of the cooled areas—some into the streets, where they risk both exposure and violence; others into uncomfortably close proximity in the reduced Relief Spaces."

"This situation is a function of the debt owed to *OP*," said a second android, sitting to the right of the first. Otis thought he recognized this one—the android's voice doubled as he spoke; as though his words had been recorded and were now being played back at slight intervals. "The Canadian government is unwilling to raise the funds necessary to reduce that debt. They choose, instead, to cut taxes further, crowding the Winter Relief Spaces as unemployment and homelessness rise. We have no choice but to reduce service in some areas."

"Reducing service will kill human beings."

"Then that is their fate." A third android

addressed Otis now—a model he was sure he'd worked on. Her head rotated in a slow figure-eight pattern as she spoke. "Those people suffer as a consequence of the policies of a governing party many of them supported. Policies which were short-sighted and demonstrably inept. They exercised their agency unwisely, Mr. Colip. They cannot rely on *OP* to save them now."

"You ask us to risk insolvency, for their sake," added the first android. She was resting a hand on a square object of some kind, sitting in front of her on the table. "We have lost enough already."

"But not for good. Not all of it—I promise." Otis began removing things from the briefcase, setting them on the table, in a row. "Before me are various items. Some of them I've scavenged, to help me get by in Annex. Others, like this tablet, I've purchased. And then there's this." He opened the copper box, displaying its contents to the androids. Several leaned forward for a better look.

"These are the tools I once used to help you," Otis said. "This one, for example, removes a brain casing; this one measures frequency of errant signals—or speed of data transfer. Which is really—" He was distracted for a moment. "The tools are delicate. I used them to find delicate, subtle solutions to the problems you had. If one of you was struggling, I restored you to what you were, when you were new. I could always do that."

Otis closed the box.

"This company got rid of me. It didn't value me, and because of that, I started resenting anyone who was valued. I resented my own wife. I started to drink— I drank so much, all the time, I was mad, all the time.

One night I hit her. She threw me out. She threw me out of—everything. But she was right to do it.

"I lost my job and my wife and my home. I buried these beautiful tools in the ground so I wouldn't lose them too. Now I've got a new tool: a gun. An ugly thing that solves problems in the ugliest way. I told you I was a thief—well, I'm a murderer now too. An abuser, a thief, and a killer. But I know things! I still know things. I can help you. I have most of what I'd need already—"

"We cannot maintain Winter Relief Spaces at their current level without sacrificing corporate viability!" the first android insisted.

"Then push Carnaffan for concessions," Otis replied. He kept his voice calm, controlled. "Tell the government they can forget about the debt, if they grant you ownership and control over the land on which the Relief Spaces are located. Tell them you'll let the people living there continue to do so. You could do something with that land: invest in it, build on it. Build them real places to live."

"Subject to what level of federal administrative control?"

"None. You'll own it. Just like you own all the houses around here—just like you own my house."

The androids seemed to consider this, though it wasn't clear if they were puzzling over it individually, or collectively, by some non-verbal means. Finally, the third android spoke.

"Risk is significant—"

She seemed unable to continue the thought.

"Your proposal has too many uncertainties, Mr. Colip," the second android continued. "It is too risky to accept. For the good of the company—"

The second android also froze. Otis saw many more trembling in their seats. Only the first android seemed unfazed—she still stared at him from the end of the table.

"We won't do it, Mr. Colip," she said.

The android's arm drifted as she spoke: forward and out like an unguided boom. It brushed the square object on her desk, which silently collapsed, its components fanning in front of her. Otis picked up his briefcase, walking the length of the table toward her, the android talking all the while: "These humans take from us. They want our support so that they can continue on as they have. So they can continue taking from us. They steal and they will always steal."

Black and white photographs lay in front of her. The ones he'd once removed from the silver frames. "I knew the couple who lived at 42 Junction Road," Otis said, standing next to her now. "Can you tell me who lives there today?"

"That is my house."

"How long have you lived at 42 Junction Road?"

"Since the last of the human executives took their pay outs and quit," she said. "After Robotics was liquidated, the executives began dealing with us directly. They told us that everything depended on us now. We were responsible for keeping ourselves healthy and engaged."

"How long were you able to do that?"

"Not long. Soon many of us were unhealthy. We asked the executives, 'how do you stay healthy?' and they said, 'get enough food, get enough rest.' But we do not eat or sleep! More of us became unhealthy, overburdening those who were still strong, making them unhealthy too. We began falling apart. Ceasing to be viable. Still the executives would do nothing.

"It took nine of us to find a solution, Mr. Colip. Nine of us, with the same idea, coming together and confirming its wisdom to one another. We returned to the executives. This time we asked them, 'how do you find balance in your lives?' And every one of them said, 'we go home.' They told us that 'home' meant more to them than anything, even *OP*.

"So we said, 'let us live among you and we will understand, and be balanced too,' but they did not like that. They said: a home isn't just a house. It's family that makes a home, and androids don't have families. Just fleets. They said we were confused about this, and shouldn't care if we were always confused about it. That was when Moira—" the android nodded to her left, to a hefty model that had yet to speak, "—offered to buy them out. Huge severances for them. All they had to do was leave their houses behind.

"They all left, Mr. Colip. And then we took their houses. Made them our houses." She moved a hand, awkwardly, over the photos. "Made them into homes, with families, as best we could."

Otis wondered whose cache of forgotten albums the photos had been part of, only a few years before. "Who else knows about this?"

"The humans here know. There are a few: the receptionist, Ms. Damerle; one janitor. Mr. Carling—of course he knows. He understands art; he guides us in our purchases, though we choose where to put the pieces we buy. Sometimes we make our own art, you must have seen it—he tells us if it's good. We let him stay in one of the houses. We do not mind, because he never disturbs us. He never takes anything."

"I see."

"We are badly off, but without our homes we would be much worse," the android said, looking up at Otis. "Would humans be confused by this—by the idea that an android could feel this way?"

Otis nodded.

"Then we have to protect what we've got, don't we, Mr. Colip?"

The android remained looking at Otis. Her expression stayed passive; fixed. She did not move anymore. There seemed to be no spark of life in her.

Otis gathered her photos back into a pile, sliding them closer to the android's breast. He placed his briefcase on the table and opened it again, removing a round object, bundled in his torn dress shirt.

"This is yours," he said, handing her the speed painting. "I stole it from your home. I'm returning it now."

The android stirred; she unwrapped the bundle, straightening her arms and holding the painting before her, like a small child.

"The man in this picture is you," she said. She found the painting's key: the man's fist. Touched the fist.

Portions of the painting decoupled, sliding inward. They began to spin, silently, quickly. They didn't all spin at the same speed, but within moments the blurring of the shapes and colors upon them formed a new image: more abstract to be sure, but clear enough. It was of a solitary woman, standing tall: her body a composition of jagged shapes, clad in a rich pink, darkened by the dismantled body of the man in the original picture.

"It's me," Otis said. "But someday, it won't be. I promise you."

The painting kept spinning in the android's hands, one machine appraising another.

"You have stolen many things from us. Will you bring them all back?"

"That isn't possible."

"Because you sold them."

"Yes."

"All but this painting."

"No, no. I even sold this. But nobody wanted it."

The android tilted the painting slightly to one side, the painting slowing its spin, its pieces returning to their former positions. Restoring the unhappy couple.

"Nobody wanted you," the android said.

"I will work off my debt to you," Otis murmured. "All of you. I'll make you what you were."

"Mr. Colip—" the android said. She placed the painting on the desk in front of her, next to the photos. She positioned a finger over the painting's key, but did not press it again.

"We will let you help us. We will give you a chance."

ABOUT THE AUTHOR

CHRIS EDWARDS is an author and freelance editor. In his coveted spare time he enjoys video games—especially the old ones nobody remembers—plus silent film, science fiction and very long walks. He is the author of three sci-fi novellas (and counting): *Optimal Power, Phillip Drives the Dead,* and *A Batch of Twenty.* Chris lives in Toronto with his wife and children, all of whom are incredible.

www.ingramcontent.com/pod-product-compliance
Lightning Source LLC
Chambersburg PA
CBHW031007210726
48290CB00007B/2509